Hanna Abi Akl

a Novel

WATERTON
PUBLISHING COMPANY
watertonpublishing.com

Dedication

This body of work is presented as fiction so it is dedicated to its characters.

To Diane, for re-introducing me to love, life, and music. And for always believing that something beautiful can come out of my madness.

To my Father, the greatest accountant in the world.

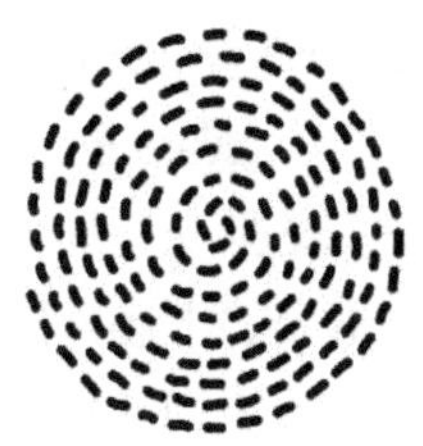

1

BUZZZ. BUZZZ. BUZZZ.

The phone buzzed next to me.

BUZZZ. BUZZZ.

BUZZZZZ.

I didn't answer. It was my editor again. He wanted to talk about my book again.

I didn't have time for him. Right now I had the phone next to me and I was staring at the white page thinking of the next great line I was about to write.

I didn't have time for distractions—even if they came in praise. A shower of praise for my latest invention. My latest book release. But lately that was all I'd been hearing about. My editor didn't sleep, but did that mean I shouldn't sleep either?

Who's going to prepare for the next great book if my thoughts were always reserved by my editor?

Anyway, the pages didn't come today. It's been a slow one, much like this weather outside.

I decided it was time for a walk. In trying times, I preferred to rest my brain rather than exhaust it, conserve the writing juice to be able to move it more freely later.

The city was slow today. With all the gloom and doom that came with the bad weather, Paris had never looked bigger. Each time I took to the streets I saw them expanding, filling more and more and more till they became infinite. It made living in this city like walking around in a never-ending labyrinth.

I went into a coffee shop—just another one I randomly picked out of the many ones lined up next to each other. I never really had a mechanism to pick out places, but having so many made it really difficult to distinguish any of them.

I had change in my pocket—2 euros and 30 cents—enough for a black. I'd never bothered checking the menu or memorizing other options because they were hardly ever available to me. My choice was usually dictated by my pocket, and it didn't come with a sophisticate taste.

The barman had a smirk drawn up the side of his face. But it quickly turned into a grunt if the customer was not bar-friendly: if he lagged by the door, took too much time to pick a seat (or sit), pointed at menu items and asked for explanations or just tried to strike up a chat in general. And of course, if he paid with big bills and had to be returned a big amount of change. Basically, the barman hated customers that required maintenance.

Me, I usually entered and looked at the first available spot. That became my seat. There was never anything special about it—but I generally grew into it while drinking the black. And by black I meant the color not the substance. That was what a couple of euros could get you in a big country.

I checked the phone again. It had been ringing and left me 2 new missed calls. The editor had been relentless with me these past few weeks, and even switching my thing to silent couldn't make me forget him for a day.

A young punk approached me. He was asking for a smoke.

'Sorry, I don't smoke,' I said. 'Had to quit ever since I became famous.'

'You're famous?' He asked. I caught the little surprise in his tone.

'Yes, yes,' I told him. 'I'm a big-time writer. I'm currently finalizing my poetry book. My editor's working on it.'

He shrugged and walked away. The little punk. This town was full of them and they were always the first species you met when you came into a new country. They carried all the vices and false ideals and false hopes, and no matter how much I convinced myself I would avoid them, I always found myself in the presence of one or two.

Outside the café window sirens were chasing cars up and down the street. The rain splattered on the asphalt and the population breathed heavily. They were tired, tired faces. The city was full of them.

I took out a book. I always carried a book with me. There was something solemn about being able to drink coffee and read a book in a small café. It was something I indulged in and, to some extent, one of the most sophisticated pleasures I allowed myself.

The pages smelled crisp. They brought back the old library book smell. I took a good whiff and looked like a drug-addict about to get high.

'Excuse me sir, are you done?'

I popped my head up and it was the barman standing over my shoulder. He was here to rob me of my alone time, of the simple pleasure I craved occasionally when days were too slow or weak for my soul.

'Uh-huh,' I told him. And I nodded my head obediently to avoid his fury or worse—being labeled a bad customer.

I paid him the money I owed and felt my pocket to make sure I didn't have any loose change I forgot about. I exited the place with no money.

Another ring. It was my editor again, still determined to reach me and discuss my book. There were still loose ends to tie up before publication: a layer of editing, a cover image (because illustrations were so abstract and didn't sell as much, my editor said) and the author's name on the book. Yes, all the big writers had fancy names: Rilke, Hugo, Sartre—they all had a good ring to their name which made it hook onto the brain and stick. That was how we were able to remember them after they'd been gone for so long.

I liked to keep things simple. No fancy stuff. I told my editor I'd use a single name throughout my writing career: John Kaliba.

But that was no good, he thought. That didn't sell.

Well it was my name!

I'd been using that name ever since moving here. Longer, actually. I didn't remember when I started adopting it exactly but it saved people the confusion of mixing up my original name or having me spell it out for them every time I was called upon or had to use it for anything. It made administrative work and ordering food and coffee very tiresome. So I decided to scrape it and go with this one.

Small. Fast. Simple. It did me good even if it didn't have a unique vibe to it. My editor had to accept it.

The other things weren't so easy for me. I couldn't figure out the book cover on my own and that was why I approached an editor in the first place. It was easy for me to write a book, but when it came to packaging the content, it wasn't as clear-cut of a job.

My marketing skills simply weren't good enough for today's market, and that was all right for me. I didn't move as fast, I didn't think as fast as others. There was a time where I would wake up and start the day with 2 sets of 10 push-ups. But that was long gone now. Today the part of my body that did most of the lifting and pushing was my brain. I thought that by letting my body go (it was a bit stocky on the sides with a beer-belly dripping from the center) my thinking would become more agile. But it was still too fast for me—the city, the people, the jobs, the cars, the lives here were too fast. Even the language and the spoken words were thrown around loosely without articulation just for the sake of it.

There was no real message, no communication. It was like people were telling each other: there, I talked back, I acknowledged you and your thoughts for brief instants. Now I'm going back to my life. My bubble.

Little bubbles. Little bubbles everywhere, floating in the trains and the subways and the city halls and the hospitals and the madhouses and the jails. I was probably the only one without one. I hadn't received my bubble yet. Or were we supposed to make it ourselves? I could never tell.

Just like I couldn't tell what would make a good cover image for my book.

But then again, that was why I hired an editor in the first place.

Oh shit, he was calling me again…

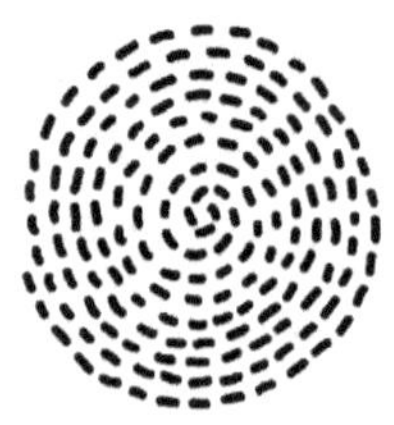

2

'**Ah, it's you again.**'

'John, why aren't you taking my calls?'

'I've been busy.'

'John, this isn't funny. Why haven't you been taking my calls?'

'I told you, I've been busy. I've been working on my next big work.'

'Have you been writing again?'

'No, but someone's got to think it before it's written down.'

'John, we have a deadline. You know damn well this book has to be done in a short window. We've already set a schedule for the book signing and we can't present something that hasn't been released yet!'

'Yeah, yeah.'

'Right. Good to hear you're motivated. We need to schedule a conference call with the visuals and graphics people for the cover. You have to be in that call. We need your take on the vision we're adopting for the book. We need to decide what we're going with.'

'Yeah, yeah.'

'Great. I'll call you with the details.'

CLICK.

For Christ sakes, I thought. My editor was an executive. He wore shiny suits and owned a big desk and worked in a big firm. He used words like 'Sharp' and 'Vision'. Words that meant nothing to me. Words you'd find on ad campaigns.

Anyway, my rent was due and my landlady had been knocking on my door for the past week. I was already god-knows-how-many-days late for the rent. She had my keys but she liked to rattle me before starting a confrontation. It was, I thought, her way of warning me or scaring me or prompting me to conjure the money I didn't have to pay her.

Anyhow, I didn't have the money. I also didn't have a job which didn't do me any good in a not-so-chaotic country. Where I came from, a man could get away with no work and living on the streets sucking beer bottles for the rest of his life. Some might even consider it daring or noble survival.

Well, out here it was plain dumb. People were treated like tokens. The country was a long line of administrative tasks, and each individual was successfully inserted into the system upon completing them. Once they'd chalked every paper, every card, every receipt off your list you were basically an integrated member of society benefiting from standard human rights like healthcare.

This meant no exceptions—not even for hotshot artists like me. After digging through dirt and mud to come up with my first book, it felt good to finally be called a writer. That feeling lasted about a week before I moved here to chase the limelight and the upper-class society where secret gatherings of famous people happened on fancy rooftops and everyone dressed in clothes they normally couldn't afford and spoke with deep refined reverberating voices that gave away much more about them than there really was.

But I was a determined son-of-a-bitch. I was a beast that had to claw to come up here and stand on that golden mountain top. I was hell-bent on going through the walls and making my name known and heard and have it passed around in cafés and bars by important people.

France was good to me in that aspect. It showed me that anybody planning to be somebody had to step up and walk around these neighborhoods, keep up with the language and embrace the culture. Which wasn't hard to do for me—even if it meant restraining myself from punching punks mocking my appearance or stance in the train in a language they called their own and thought I was estranged from.

Another notion to keep in mind was the paperwork. In a country that had invented smart systems that could plan your entire day for you or schedule reservations on your behalf, paperwork was still widely regarded as the official recourse. Everything worth knowing was written (sometimes printed) and stamped. Which was why I had a nice stack of papers in my room from my landlady.

One of them stated that the rent was due before the 7th of the month. The others were hand-written notes from her asking about overdue rent:

Hello, this is to remind you your rent's due this month. Please settle your payment as soon as possible. Thank you.

Hello, your rent is overdue. Please settle the payment as soon as possible.

The rent is overdue. Settle as soon as possible.

A tip for the untrained eye: the shorter the note, the more severe it was. After a while the introductions were dumped altogether and the message just looked like a plain threat.

I never understood why my landlady went through so much trouble with the letters. Was it because she was part of the system and taught to do so? It would have been much easier for her to barge in on me and kick me out. Relieve me from my strain and pain and haste of waiting for the day my eyes matched hers in the lobby. But then, I would have no place to go, in a country I didn't know. Is this the bittersweet end of a writer-in-the-making? Or is it to be the perilous ride of a phenomenal craftsman in a meteoric rise?

Either way, I needed cover. I needed to keep myself safe, to tend to my worrying brain and soul, to get rid of the jitters that accompanied me from dusk till dawn. I needed some security.

And here that word was synonymous to one thing: money. And that overshadowed getting a job, being employed, working in a place with people you disliked at things that didn't matter—to you at least.

It wasn't an unfamiliar route for me, and I had been down that trodden path before, albeit without much success. I was never really good at anything, never really interested in developing a skill or learning to communicate with people.

I was at ease on my own. And I knew that kind of thinking was condemned and banished in an open world where everything was linked and everyone was connected to everyone, but it just felt better for me to stay on my island and distance myself.

And no, no, no, this is not another sad tale of a failed man or writer-wannabe trying to grind it out like the rest of them. Yes, yes, I'd read all the books, the great and mediocre ones, I'd seen how writers were portrayed and slayed and burned for leading unpleasant (often demoralizing) crude lives. I was not trying to emulate that stereotype. I was simply a clever man that could put down some clever lines yet to be acknowledged by the general community. But my time would come. I could feel it. It took time to engineer good words and good writing and it also took time to put together a good life. But I was working on that. Like I said, I was a determined son-of-a-bitch living in a small room drinking lots of coffee and beer with a book to my name.

3

I**T WAS NOON WHEN** I woke up in a familiar bed. The sheets were washed and perfumed with a delicate aroma and looked pearly white.

I tasted stale coffee in my mouth. It reminded me how I ended up here: last night after coming face to face with myself that I would never be able to pay my rent, or own up my failure to do so to my wicked landlady like a proper man, I stormed out of my apartment and came knocking on my girlfriend's door.

I told her I decided to hide out at her place and see out my dark days until I found a resolution to my problems.

'What about your book?' She asked me.

'What about it?'

'How's the publishing process going?'

'Slow.'

'Did you talk to your publisher about it?'

'I'm trying not to.'

'You're unbelievable. How do you expect things to work out for you if you don't put any effort in them and just sit there and drink and eat and complain? Look at me when I am talking to you and stop sipping on that goddamn coffee!'

To be fair she knew what she was talking about. She was a good girl I met not long after coming here and who saw through my genius since day one. She also saw through the crazy dancing straws of madness that came with it and welcomed them with open arms. She was a good, talented and hard-working soul who could just as well sit down with the best artistic minds and talk up big literary ideas or criticize Renaissance paintings.

I could understand her passionate warning cry and her desire to shake me to get off my ass and do something about my faltering life here. She had managed to get a job not long after she arrived here and was pretty good at it. To be honest I never understood it too well to go into much detail about it, but I knew enough to realize it made her happy. It made her feel accomplished and gave her hopes and big dreams. It gave her confidence and courage.

But here she was wrong. The same logic couldn't be applied to my case because, well, I had just come off writing a BIG BIG book that would soon go down as a best-seller and re-evoke memories of the Beats and the romantics and the existentialists all put together. It had the pizzazz and flair of the great books written by some of the biggest literary names. So as far as I was concerned I had done my time. I had put in the effort. What were France and life and the literary community waiting for to acknowledge my work? It didn't seem fair. None of it did.

It wasn't fair for me to have my dirty laundry in a store bag instead of a laundry basket. It wasn't fair for me to have to shower standing in a hole without a shower curtain or a drain to suck out the water splashing all around. It wasn't fair for me to be sleeping in a room that was always—always—cold with no heater or warm bedsheets.

The world was against me. It was always too quick to crucify its artists and martyrize them. It was some kind of bittersweet tribute to the minds that were hell-bent on defying norms and producing, producing content that killed normality and everything it rubbed off on.

She couldn't see it. With all her wits and smarts she expected me to fall into place, to chain myself to a system that was malfunctioning by the day, to file in with my fellow human beings: the butcher, the baker, the train station agent—and depend on them.

Well, I didn't need anyone to write a goddamn book. I didn't see why I would need anyone to hold my hand and walk me through the trenches of this shark lane full of hungry predators.

But of course, I didn't tell her that. The person in me despised confrontation, especially with her. She had a way to turn any man's best arguments against him, and transform any ongoing debate into a psychological evaluation session where he would take notes of his faults and pledge to work on bettering himself.

It was part of her strength, hitting back hard against people and giving them a good slap in the character to make them better. But it was also part of my weakness. I hated arguments. I hated disagreements. I hated fights. I wasn't good in any of them, except maybe on paper since I was comfortable with words and using them.

So I got up and poured myself a cup of coffee. The house was empty. My girl was probably taking her 10-minute timed lunch break (they were allowed an hour, but she liked to rush through it to get back to work quickly). I opened the curtains and let the blazing sun blast me full-face. It was golden like the grass in the little parks in the surrounding area or the fur of every dog being walked by its owner.

But I looked at the people. They were miserable. They were all angry with themselves or with someone else. They were walking in straight lines, unshifting, unwavering, carrying their phones and making angry grimaces at them. They cried because of words said or unsaid, of unspoken sentences they were hoping to hear, or a piece of good news they were waiting for in their mailbox—even getting up on Sundays to check for—that would never come.

I didn't share their pain. I didn't share the pain of the children being bombarded in the region I came from, I didn't share the cry of the Arabs, the liberty chants of the good and the gay and the faithful, the audacity of the newcomers with a champions' mentality to pioneer and innovate and excel in a foreign country harboring average hopes for the lot of them, or at the very least, the majority of them.

My phone rang. A quick look at the incoming picture on the screen told me it wasn't my publisher and put my fears at ease. It was Diane.

'Hey, baby. You up?'

'Uh-huh.'

'Had your coffee?'

'Uh-huh.'

'What's your day like?'

I stared at the sun again. 'Blind and irritating so far,' I said.

'You're always so dramatic about everything. Anyway, I'll be home around 6 and I'll grab some groceries on the way. Do you need anything in particular?'

'I'm good.'

She kissed me over the phone and hung up. There were many things in life I didn't believe in, but love was still something I wasn't completely decided on. I was able to share simple nights with this girl, pouring cheap wine in plastic goblets and chugging them while listening to jazz music. That made me happy.

I decided to lean on love to help me see out the day more clearly. I sat drinking more coffee and waiting for the kiss she sent me over the phone.

It never arrived.

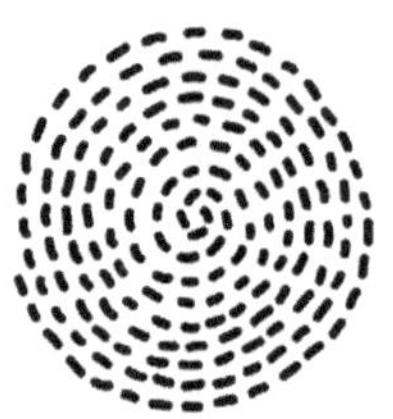

4

Paris was as welcoming as the next city on the map. For everything it had to offer in terms of tall buildings and monuments, museums of rare art and hidden words, the people always flocked around the simplest things.

It was true: most of them chose to get excited about food—the next food place that would open in the vacant space next to the market, the next culinary experience around the block, the next fancy burger recipe promising a unique taste for an out-of-budget price.

I visited the city on multiple occasions—multiple times to get away from the boredom that chased me around and cornered me in various tight spots, to let loose the little thoughts that wandered in my mind (like how tall the Eiffel tower really was), to feed on the power of walking down the same streets ancient writers walked some ages ago. Most of the time I wished those trips would reward me with something—like a little writing juice to churn away at and splatter all over my white pages (virgin, virgin pages I called them). But I thought a big part of writing was patience, or at this point, plain old wishing. Diane loved the city. She especially loved the green spots and had a good knack for finding them. They looked like their own little habitats, some sort of reclusive sites that took you in and enclosed themselves like oysters, swallowing you and carrying you as far away from the world and the cars and the cursing and the people and the buses and the mercenaries and the homeless and the priests and the troubled and the scholars.

'Look at the sky,' she told me.

I stared at the vast blue space.

'Look at its colors.' She smiled and her lips released something pure, something real, something worth touching and being touched by.

I never really took the time to notice things. As a writer, you were taught—or discovered by your means—that most of your work relied on observation and the study of things around you. It was a skill most craftsmen boasted or bragged about or showed off. Some were even endorsed for jobs for possessing it. I never really picked up on that skill and never felt the need to. It never came in the way of my writing, of my seeing and understanding of what twisted and turned and endeavored in my surrounding. But being with Diane made me realize it was more a way of life than a skill. You see, friend, things went bad constantly and drew sick scathing images in our thoughts. But in between there were moments—sparse little intervals of ecstasy and fulfillment—that gathered some of life's best attributes and put them on display for us. It was a way of reaching out, a proof of existence of something naturally good that coursed through the underground tunnels, passing by the late-night bars and restaurants and insurance companies and auto-rental shops and courtyards and riverbanks.

Diane was willing to listen and identify them. She saw explosive colors streaming live from skylines, exuberant sunsets colored by shades of pink and orange and yellow, and rainbows forming in the middle of parks during rain showers.

'Sometimes,' she said, grabbing my hand, 'I feel like we're not alone in this world.'

'It's hard for me to accept that.'

'How come?'

'Because we are born alone and we die alone. And anyone who believes in god or a higher power is searching for ways to cover up an unshakable truth: we are alone. Mankind is alone. There is no god or higher form or merciful being or larger purpose. We are born like this, into this and we spend our days filling ourselves until our bodies grow tired and weary and decay and are buried in the ground.'

'And what will you do, if you ever find out that there is a god? That there is a mystical being waiting for you after death?'

'Baby, if that's the case, then I'll be happy to sit and have a beer with him. I have a list of questions for him.'

There were no particularly good days for me. None that I really looked forward to or preferred over others. But Sundays were best because they were the days Diane was forced to take time off work and we could get out of the house and hide away in a nice park and get carried away by existential discussions that never fully satisfied either of our curious minds. Sundays were also the only days my publisher was tied to his family and had to spend his days out of the office. They were the only days he had to shift his attention away from me and left me alone from book-related details I didn't want to hear about.

'Just publish, goddamit!' I told him the last time I took his bloody call.

'We still have to arrange a meeting with the guys, we still have planning to do for the release, we need to start thinking about the book signing…'

Planning, thinking, calling, speaking. None of those were doing. I was an unhappy writer who felt his fame was being held back by incompetence and laziness. A fidgeting force was holding back all my power and talent and I didn't like it. I wanted the book published, released and distributed so that it could circulate among the few interesting minds that still took pride in reading a paperback or quoting philosophers whose names were too challenging for me to pronounce without stuttering.

'I won't make it,' I told Diane.

She put down her wine. 'Why do you think that, baby?'

'I just won't make it.'

'You'll make it.'

'I won't, the odds are too great.'

'You'll make it, I believe in you. Someday you'll be a great writer, a printed writer, a quoted writer. Perhaps even a messenger or a beacon people will cling onto when they have nothing else to hope for.'

'Baby,' I told her, 'the world is terrible enough without me. I don't think I can save it but I think I can chase down some of the rot in it. I think what I write makes sense, to me at least, and I think it will make sense to others. Maybe there are people like me out there, people who think and act and behave and believe like me. People who understand the world the way I do and who just need a flash from me to congregate and gravitate toward each other.'

'When will you stop ignoring your publisher? You can't run away from him forever. Besides, it's not right. He has an important say in your book and you need him. You can't get this book through on your own. Think about that, if the book is really that important to you. Think about that if you care.'

Then she went back to sipping her wine. I drank mine in gulps and poured some more.

'You drink fast,' she said. 'You drink too fast.'

'I know,' I said.

The moonlight crept in on us. The day spent in Paris was a long foregone memory now. The cluttered furniture in the apartment were overcome by black shades striding through the balcony glass. I thought about an underground dungeon or safe house to contain us both from the world. Everything was hostile. I couldn't shake off the feeling of vigilance I developed and that started to wear on me like a shell. I couldn't let down my guard and accept that the modern world was much more forgiving than previous ones. There was a hard pressing against my chest, a pressing only writing could sooth. That and getting in bed with Diane and listening to instrumental jazz music flowing across the room or switching to classical piano and imagining the stroking of the keys being pushed down and surging back up again.

Ah, the magic. The magic. The magic. The wine was good and the last train had set in the station a few minutes away from where we lived. I still owed the world a lot of things. But a voice told me I was getting there, and that one day I would call the shots and take my head out of the lion's bite.

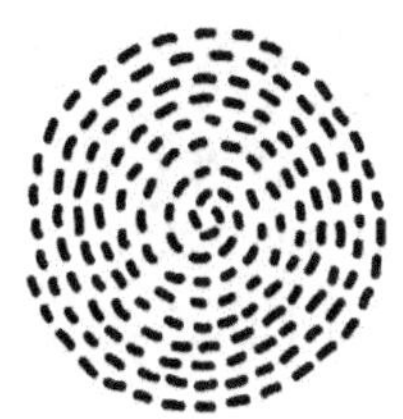

5

THE NEXT MORNING I decided to go out into the city. Diane had given me some money, and having her working all day meant I was resigned to spending my time alone at home or dodging more calls from my guy.

I took the train to the capital. I had to squeeze my way in before the mechanical doors shut mercilessly on every living being standing on the thin line separating the platform from the train.

Inside the people shoved each other even more robotically to create space for themselves. I received pushes, elbows, kicks and even snarls from one bad-breathed old fucker stapled against my back. That only made me hate the human race even more and grow more and more uneasy during the ride.

Zombies. These people were like zombies. They walked across the platforms and inserted their tickets through the booths like a brainwashed crowd. That was what it took to be part of a working system: giving up any kind of freedom and uniqueness to fit the model. Any person that stopped to fidget would stir the others and cause uproar. Any person who tilted his head while waiting in line would cause a huge commotion.

It was true: the government gave you everything—food, job, security, healthcare. The part they didn't mention was that they took your thinking in exchange.

Anyhow, I made it into the city and started looking for a coffee place. I had some change in my pocket but the rattling they made lured me into a false hope that I had enough money to buy out a day in an expensive city.

Those hopes were quickly dashed, however, when I finally stopped at a place run by an Algerian shop owner. I had visited this place quite a few times before (and broken my unspoken rule of never trying out the same coffee shop more than once) and was seen as some kind of regular in the eyes of the man in charge. He was a friendly guy in general, especially toward his kind, but in terms of business his prices were just as harsh as any typical French bistro.

I took out the coins from my pocket and carefully counted them on one of the tables. My suspicions were correct: I had just enough money to treat myself to a coffee here plus a dried-out ham-and-cheese sandwich from the nearest supermarket.

'Hello my friend,' the Algerian greeted me. 'Long black as usual?'

I nodded politely and took a corner seat. His welcoming interactions did little to mask his Arabic traits. I sat and scouted his face and the more I looked at him, the more Arab he looked to me. It got me wondering how or when I started discerning people like that—when did I catch the disease that made locals here label Arab folks and other immigrants as foreigners just by looking at them?

It was the same for that Tunisian man sitting at the front table. He was also a loyal customer here and a close friend of the Algerian. I happened to know because I used to overhear their not-so-discrete conversations. The Tunisian was a brilliant mathematician trying to find a job here but was beaten by candidates with much more enviable backgrounds. Essentially what that meant was that companies often labeled profiles more favorably depending on the applicant's country of origin. For Arabs, most of whom came from war-torn countries, this made things especially difficult. The Tunisian thought so too and was always rambling about having to 'constantly and consistently prove himself' ahead of others to get a knack into the job world where he believed he was already better than most of the bunch applying for similar positions.

The Algerian listened to his rants and repeated what I thought was a pre-recorded answer to him about perseverance and hope. His answer would often take the dimension of a generalized proverb about the struggles of mankind and the importance of one's belief in a dream.

I had a hard time telling how sincere the shop owner really was, but what disheartened me was the way I was slowly buying into this local, hostile, disagreeable mentality and looking differently at the two people exchanging words at the front of the shop despite having a close cultural background to them.

It made me uneasy and I slid in my chair thinking I was a foreigner here too and that I should not forget it. At the same time, a voice was crying out inside me : YOU ARE FROM THE WEST. YOU BELONG TO THE WEST. Was it my interest and fascination with literature and art? Was it because a book captivated me more than a machine-gun?

I could feel the concept of roots and origins quickly dissolving in me. The café walls began to melt and it looked like a large cardboard box trying to hold together all these different people.

The coffee came and I drank it in one big gulp. I paid my 2.30€. On the way out, I saluted the Algerian. I remembered it was common curtesy where I came from.

Parisian clouds were dark and heavy. The sky was sucking up everything it could from dust to human souls. I walked along the street a stranger, a broke stranger, a poor stranger. Somehow I had lapsed into a sinister darkness that stepped over my impeding rise to literary fame and numbed out the satisfaction I had been feeding on from it.

I was drawn back to square one, I was thrown back into the mix with the millions and millions of foreigners that came into this country to rebuild or start fresh. It was unfair for someone like me, someone who was always destined for greatness but just needed the platform to propel him into that stratosphere, but on the larger scale I was a profile, a social security number, a tenant occupying a home I couldn't afford. They had gotten hold of me and tagged me, billed me, and withheld my abilities. The only things I could keep calling my own were my abilities to write and love.

I crossed the supermarket without going in. My brain and my stomach no longer found the dried sandwich appealing. I tried to think about my lost appetite as making savings—albeit for the wrong reasons—but here your lifeline was measured by the amount of money you held, not the food you ate. Once that figure dropped to zero, so did your turn and it was GAME OVER.

Having conceded my hunger, I looked for the nearest metro station to catch a train back home. The writer in me was wishing for instant literary fame.

The lover in me just wanted to crawl under the sheets and wait for my woman to come home.

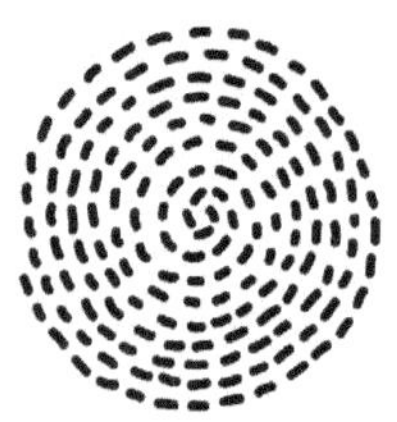

6

I MADE LOVE TO Diane that night.

Lying in bed there, alone together, was how I pictured peace. 'I'm sure most wars would stop existing if people loved each other more often,' I always told her.

She giggled to that naïve statement. Every time.

Diane had that look on her face again. That look that only showed up after we made love or whenever we were watching the sun together. That rare mysterious look that I couldn't quite put into words. Maybe it was because I still hadn't found the words for it.

It was a look that took her to another place. And it took me with her. It transported us to another universe and made me wish we'd never come back. Our hangouts there were sweet but short. We bounced off clouds and rolled in endless flower-filled prairies. We listened to bird calls—all kinds of them.

Diane bit her lip. I locked her hand in mine and ran it across her body. She was more than a woman that night. She was a place of worship.

If god himself ever intended for me to believe or restore my faith (somehow) in earthly things, then he was doing a pretty good job.

'I love you,' I said.

Diane was different from other people I'd known. She never said things in a mainstream way. She had her own manner of expressing herself.

'I love your fingers,' she said.

'Yeah?'

'Yeah. I love how you take care of them. I think a man who takes care of himself is worth loving.'

'Tell me something else you love about me.'

'Your name. I love your name.'

'I don't see how you can love somebody by their name.'

'But I do. It's so powerful.'

'I can compose symphonies with yours. Only I don't know how to make music.'

She giggled. The ends of that little laugh ricocheted against the room and brought the walls a little closer together. It would've been nice if they just closed on us, just the both of us, and sank us into some kind of tight blackness that would force us to stick our bodies together for the rest of time.

I gave my woman a kiss on the forehead and got up for a beer. 'Last one in the fridge honey,' she said.

I drank it in slow gulps and watched her wiggle her naked body in bed, slightly moving sideways to adjust herself. Whether or not she knew I was watching her movement mattered little. I very much enjoyed watching her alive.

'Honey, we're out of beer,' I told her.

'I'll grab a pack on my way home tomorrow.'

'Ok.'

'Any news from your publisher?'

'No. He hasn't been calling lately.'

'Do you think there's a problem? Do you think the book deal's off?'

'No chance, baby. I signed a contract. Besides, he needs me.'

She chuckled. 'I love you, but you're not the only writer out there.'

'I might be one of the few good ones left.'

'We'll see about that.'

She got up and wore a velvet red see-through robe. She looked very kinky.

'You know,' I told her, 'your ability to push me is unmatched by anyone else.'

'It's because I care about you. And I hate the thought of seeing your art go to waste.'

'Unfortunately, I'm a stubborn man. You should know that by now.'

'I just don't understand why you won't talk to your publisher about your damn book!'

I started shouting.

She shouted back.

We started fighting. It wasn't an uncommon thing for us to suddenly erupt like that from little starting points, especially whenever they accumulated and I had trouble recognizing it.

But it mostly came down again to my inability to pick my fights well and how bad I was at the ones I picked—that and Diane's balanced mind that always struck well between reason and emotion, whereas mine used stubbornness as combustible to run.

Luckily for both of us the fight was short. She exhausted my folly and stubbornness in no-time and asked herself out loud what was it that she saw in me.

'All writers are crazy,' I told her.

'Don't play the mercenary with me.'

'Believe me baby, all writers are crazy. It's a curse they're born with, and denying it only makes it harder to accept. But it's also part of their charm.'

In moments—in singular identifiable countable moments—I would feel that I'd lost that woman. That she was no longer on the same wavelength as me. That she no longer understood my madness or my recklessness. I noticed those moments because they broke the homogeneity we shared and split our lives in two distinct pieces.

But again, I was fortunate enough that these moments didn't last. Diane always came back. Not immediately, not naturally. She would hesitate, take a few steps, draw a line, erase it, draw another at the frontier of my world, go splash in the ocean, then come back and erase everything she drew. Finally she would step in again and restore the comfort that we'd been robbed of during our fight.

'I guess you do have a certain charm,' she said.

I smiled at her. I couldn't top that sentence. I couldn't top any of it. I remembered that in the large pile of mess I was building for myself, there had been and remained one constant: that girl right there in front of me. And something in my gut told me she would continue to be for a while at least.

And it was hard, friend. It was hard to battle so many demons that came with the word. Sometimes I thought about the struggle the outside world never perceived: being a writer meant thinking about random words at different occurrences of life and immediately feeling their weight and implication on your soul. And to have someone on board with that, to have someone sign up for a twisted ride like that and say, 'Hey, I can take that, my soul can take that, my entire being is ready to be put to that,' was a far harder feat than Diane made it seem.

And for that I felt grateful.

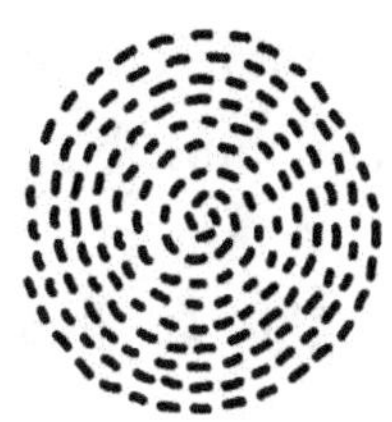

7

WITH MY NEWFOUND SENSE of appreciation, I decided to call my publisher today.

I dialed his number—that my phone screen had gotten so used to seeing by now—nervously and waited for the pickup tone.

RING. RING. RING.

'John?'

'Err, yes, this is John.'

'How are you?'

'Okay.'

'I must say I'm surprised you called.'

'Yeah, I don't much believe it myself.'

'I take it you're finally ready to talk about the book?'

'If it means getting done with this whole process…'

'Fantastic! I'm so glad to hear that! Let me just put the designers in the call. Oh, and there's also the marketing team and the shipping people and…'

'Listen, listen, I don't want to talk to anybody. These are your people and I don't give two damns about any of them. I just want to see the book done in book form. That's all I want. I don't want to worry about the details. I'll leave those headaches to you.'

'Alright.'

'Alright.'

'So why are you calling then if not for the book details?'

'I just want to hear that it will be done. My girlfriend and I are getting impatient.'

'Of course it will be done! We signed a contract!'

'That's what I told her too.'

'You can re-assure her it will be done.'

'O.k.'

'Alright. Anything else?'

'Um, no. Um, actually, one more thing. I'd like to know when the book will be out.'

'Well that depends. I still have to finalize the cover with the designers and check with the marketing people for the book launch campaign and…'

'Alright, alright. So you'll let me know.'

'Yes, yes, I'll let you know. You are the author after all.'

'Uh-huh.'

'You and your girlfriend can be reassured, John. The book will be out soon. I'm working on it!'

'O.k. I'll tell her that.'

'Great to hear you're fully committed and excited about this! I'll give the green light for the team to start working right away!'

'O.k.'

CLICK.

Man, oh man, I thought. It was a funny world. They gave you enough material to create something that could stand for a lifetime and pulled it from under your feet as soon as you had it. Then before you knew it, it was wrapped up, labeled, packaged and ready to sell. We had gone from selling utensils for the body to selling utensils for the mind. The merchandise had changed but the process had pretty much stayed the same.

Artists—they were being held and preserved to starve the masses. They were being upheld to create demand and used to supply it. They were nothing more than gap-fillers, like the eternal aisles in supermarket stores or hardware repair shops or gas stations.

I felt cheap. Cheaper than the post officer delivering the mail, cheaper than the supermarket boy bagging groceries and eggs, cheaper than the whore enslaving herself to good-paying customers who were probably far worse human beings than her.

After the phone call I took a stroll and found myself wandering into some unknown streets in Paris. The architecture was annoyingly symmetric: the streets all looked the same, just with different shop brands. It was too perfect for my taste and my already-ill sense of orientation.

In trying to find a meaningful direction I had suddenly arrived to a large esplanade ending in a circular ring-like hangout. People flocked there because it was a vantage point that strategically overlooked a large chunk of the city. From there the roofs reminded me of the everlasting symmetry this country was founded on: in its architecture, in its people, in its administration, in its food. From a ridge near the end of the hangout a different part of the city opened up to me: I saw the Eiffel tower beaming with all its colors across everything surrounding it. I thought about my book, I thought about needing to write but not wanting to, I thought about the rent money I owed my old landlady, I thought about all the signed papers I owed France and didn't bother having with me now, I thought about Diane and spending the night by her side.

Not far from me a little girl riding her scooter tripped and fell on the hard floor. She started to wail in pain while her mother, a few feet away from her and walking her other kid by the hand, heard her without reacting. She simply told the girl to pick herself up and dust off her little blue dress.

An episode like this was enough to make me forget where I was. It made me realize I could still be more human in anything I wrote than by interacting with any of these people. It made me want to see my book come alive at last, and take my place among the great writers of my time.

Things will get easier, I said to myself in a hushed voice while walking away from the people. Things will get easier when the book sees the light, when I hoist it up in the air and touch it against the unforgiving French sky or slit it in between the rays of the gigantic Parisian tower.

Things will get easier for me, for Diane, and for anything else I might care about someday. I now believe in the word more than I ever have, more than anything else, and I will drop the unnecessary things this country puts me through to vigorously chase it down and hunt it across every bakery and bookshop before it vanishes from my reach.

I turned and looked at the ring of people standing and making noises. I must leave them now, for I have become a prophet who's just received his revelation and must go on to fulfill it.

8

Things were going bad with Diane.

We'd hit a rough patch recently and couldn't get out of it. It was like digging a hole, friend, and digging and digging just to see how much we could sink.

There have been a lot of fights. Some notable ones involved throwing objects (not too heavy) and sitting in opposite corners of the room drinking our favorite bottle of alcohol.

I'd watched that girl hold onto a lot of things, but not quite like she held onto a bottle of wine. She didn't hold it with possession—like a typical drunkard would—but rather with desperation. For Diane to hold onto a bottle of wine meant depletion. It meant a human being walking toward the edge and staring down the curb. It meant the rough, rough fall that I traced in her eyes.

For my part, whiskey was my favorite pet. I always marveled at how the same product could have such varying tastes depending on the situation it was being consumed in. Like a chicken marinated sandwich at dawn after a late night out. It never tasted like the one you had at dinner before drinking (that one you could really taste the mayonnaise in), but it had its own odd flavor that reminded you where and what time it was no matter how disoriented you were.

Whiskey was no different. My friend Jack had been good to me over the years—we'd had some special times together—and he swore an oath never to let me down no matter how bad or shitty or ugly or dark matters got. Whether he expected me to do the same and promise to stick by the bottle every time things went south was something I wasn't sure of: the bottle of Jack had been with me through uncertain times, twisted mad black days of bad writing, suicidal tendencies like drowning my gut with alcohol or trying to leap out of the window or running naked on the highway. I believed those kind of things forged strong alliances because they came out of vulnerability. So I said yes to Jack, sure, I'll hold onto you a little more, a little longer then.

Back to Diane. In our latest installment, we found ourselves hitting a brick wall. Several of them, actually. Pounding our heads madly against them hoping to break through to the other side. But the only things getting smashed were our heads.

In a series of turbulent and tumultuous trials and tribulations, we argued about sex, marriage, love, smoking pot together, communication, travel, money and a lot of other shit the whiskey is omitting from my brain. On the outside, these might seem like regular topics regular couples fought over. Except it wasn't that for us. Our fights were anything but regular. We had a beautiful way of orchestrating a fight and turning it into a rumble. Not a physical one. More like the emotional ride an opera takes you through. Our fights pit soul against soul and drained us both, until Diane's body started shaking and completely shut off and I went brain-dead and still.

I still didn't understand the bible or any other holy book that talked about the way to love. About the way to forgive. Forgive thy neighbor? Really? Was it supposed to be that literally simple or simply poetic? Diane and I found a terrible time forgiving each other—so how the hell was I supposed to forgive our loud noisy neighbor (a black teenager who hosted frat parties every night while we were making love next door and got a kick out of reggae music)?

Anyhow, Diane wanted me out of the house for a while. We both thought a little distance would do us good even though we both knew it was a lie. Distance was not good—in love or in writing. Staying away from the word for too long made a writer frail and bitter—it made him unstable and a little clumsier in his judgment of things around him. But we went through with it.

I had met an Indian man and befriended him. He was the kind of guy you could always walk in on and find him surrounded by a cloud of thick white smoke—right there in the centerpiece of his one-room apartment in Paris. He also had a French girlfriend who lived not far from him and whom he hooked up with constantly (when he wasn't sleeping with his other Indian girlfriend). Anyhow, the Indian man, for all his recklessness and uncertainty, found his way into my skin and grew on me.

Conveniently, now that I wasn't in my drunken haze of whiskey and foul-mouth attitude, I distinctly remembered him talking up wanting to leave his apartment to go live with his girlfriend (the French one). So I decided to sit with the man, seeing as though I suddenly found myself needing a place to stay in.

I took the train from Diane's place to Paris. My Indian friend was waiting for me for lunch in an Indian place. I wasn't too big on Indian food, but hey, I knew I wasn't allowed to be picky this time.

Asking for a place to stay was as demeaning as running out of food—if not more. We humans were not blessed like the mighty tortoise to carry our houses on our backs at all times and just decide to camp in them whenever we pleased. We weren't equipped either with as much survival instinct; or I wasn't, in all cases. I liked to think I was a pretty analytical man and had reasonably good assessment skills when it came to any kind of situation, but I must admit I didn't have a stronghold on the housing and living matter.

Cue the Indian man. The train dropped me a few blocks away from the meeting place and I dragged myself under the swift light diagonal rain hitting me in the cheekbones. I was also low on cash so I figured if my luck was any good, he'd offer me lunch.

I had no trouble recognizing his face without the clot of white smoke hanging above it. He greeted me with his characteristic smirk that always puzzled me and could be hiding extreme contentment or ire at any time.

'Nice to be seeing you, my friend,' he started off.

'Yeah, you too.'

'So as I understand you'll be needing a place to stay?'

'Yeah.'

'And are you looking for something specific?'

'Just a floor and a sleeping area. A bathroom would be good too.'

'Then I might be able to help you.'

'Yeah.'

'I believe you're familiar with the place I'm currently occupying.'

'Uh-huh.'

'Well, I'll be moving out very soon to live with my girlfriend on a permanent basis.'

'Ok.'

'The place is yours if you want it.'

'Ok.'

'Is there anything in particular you'd like to ask about?'

'Yeah, actually. How's your landlady?'

He looked dumbfounded at me. 'Um, that's not the kind of question I was expecting. I'm not sure what you mean by that.'

'I mean, is she a bitch?'

'Um, I'm not sure. No. I don't really know.'

'Ok.'

'How's yours?'

'She's a walking, talking whore.'

'To be honest, I'm kind of lost here. I thought we were talking about the apartment...' he let out a few nervous laughs.

'Oh, but we are. And it's very important to me to know what your landlady's like. How about you describe her for me.'

'Well, she's an old retired woman who has a keeper come in and take care of her. That's the same person in charge of cleaning all the apartments in the neighborhood where I live. The landlady pops up on Saturdays to check up on the residents but other than that, we don't really see her much.'

'Ok. And rent?'

'Oh, she never asks for it. She has someone taking care of that for her because she gets quite forgetful.'

'I see. And who is this person exactly?'

'Just some middle-aged man. He wears glasses and shows up once a month to collect the money. For some reason he always wears a suit. He just passes by and knocks on every door and greets everyone with a huge smile on his face and asks for the rent money.'

'Uh-huh.'

'John, why are you asking me all this? Do you think you'll have any problem paying the rent?'

'No, no. I just want to get a feel for the place I'll be living in.'

His eyes stopped meeting mine from that moment. You could tell when human beings start being uncomfortable or stressed or uncertain by some unmissable signs. He closed down his face and tried hard to contain any awkward emotion that was running through him. I knew my questions were harried and weird, but I wasn't sorry for any of them. I was a defenseless man, an easy target for an unforgiving world, and I wanted to be damn sure I wasn't about to enter a hostile environment like the one I got out of in my previous apartment. I didn't intend to become food for the lions by moving to the center of Paris.

My Indian friend sunk his face in his hot curry plate and started eating rapidly. He functioned with keen Indian precision and optimization. Those people amazed me by how automated they could be in everything they did. For my part, I had trouble getting through most of my plate simply because I didn't enjoy that kind of food. What really helped me more than the hunger was knowing in fact this might well be my only meal for the day.

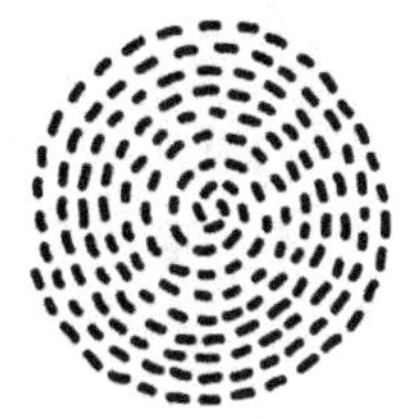

9

'SO YOU'LL TAKE IT?' the Indian asked.

'I guess so.'

'Great. There's one thing I should warn you about though.'

'What's that?'

'The shower's broken. But the good news is the landlady is aware of it and she's sending someone over to fix it in the next couple of days.'

'How long has it been broken?'

'A while now.'

'And why hasn't it been fixed before?'

'Like I told you, she forgets.'

'And you didn't remind her?'

'I was spending most of my time at my girlfriend's place anyways.'

'Uh-huh.'

'One more thing.'

'Tell me.'

'The bed.'

'Is it broken too?'

'No, but it does make a few squeaky noises when you move a lot in it. They said they were going to change it too.'

'Right. Anything else?'

'You might want to consider investing in a lamp. The place is rather badly lit.'

'The darkness doesn't bother me.'

We finished up. The Indian tore into his plate like a razor slicing bushes in its path. I was able to progress well into mine but barely made it to the finish line. There's only so much curry a man can take.

The Indian beat me to the punch and called for the bill. To ensure my plan would be executed faultlessly, I insisted on paying.

'Let me get that one,' I said.

'No, man, it's fine. We'll split it.'

'No, really, I insist. It's the least I could do for your troubles coming in here and meeting me.'

'Man, you're crazy. It's no trouble at all.'

'Really, it's the least I could do. And for the house and everything. You're really saving me here.'

'No, no, if anything you're getting out of the rut. The least I could do is help you out.'

The bill came and the whole payment thing was still up in the air.

'Can I ask you a question, John?' my Indian friend said.

'Fire away.'

'Why do you dislike your landlady so much?'

'Let's just say we didn't see eye to eye, me and her.'

'How's that?'

'She wanted me to pay rent and I didn't want to.'

'HAHA, you're a funny man, John!'

He took out his wallet. He opened it and started slashing the paper bills inside.

'You know what, today's on me! Lunch with you put me in a really good mood!'

'That's really nice of you.'

He settled the full thing and handed me his keys.

'The place's a bit dirty and needs some dusting and a bit of cleaning, but it's not a mess. I already took out my stuff from there,' he said.

'I think I'll manage. Thanks again.'

'Don't mention it. I have a gorgeous French hottie waiting for me in her apartment and I'm going to make love to her right now until she screams and her lungs pop out of her chest.'

'That's good. By the way, what happened to that other Indian girl?'

'She's still there. I see her on weekends.'

'Ok. Well thanks again for the house and everything.'

He went his way. I got out of the restaurant and the rain had stopped. A little shy sun was peeking from the sky and I decided things were okay for now. I followed the directions to my new apartment and managed to get there without too much trouble.

When I arrived, I discovered two things: first, that the Indian had lied and the place was a mess. It was unlivable with the residual *hash* on the table and mountains of dust piled on every surface. There was also a pair of dirty boxer shorts left out in one of the drawers. Second, the place was so poorly lit it made it difficult for me to do anything, even grab a piece of old cloth and clean. This kind of darkness was something I wasn't accustomed to and something I didn't like. It was different from the darkness I perceived when I was hiding in bed with Diane with all the lights off. I decided I didn't like this type of darkness, that I wanted a similar darkness to the one I was used to with that girl.

Out there it was still daylight, but it was not my world. This had become my world: dark, lonely and dirty. A triumphant new beginning for the newborn writer who was adamant to take over the world with his talent and prowess.

I could hear the echo of chants bursting through the apartment walls depicting the loser that had come to be and reside within them. What would save me now? Knowing that my book would be published and born into this world? Trying to mend things with the woman I loved? Basking in the fact that I lived in the center of one of the most reputable cities in the world?

All those things seemed sadly unequally weighted, and sadder still that none of them filled my empty cups. There was no food in this place, but clean water running from the kitchen faucet, so I could at least drink without feeling any kind of disorientation.

The only right thing left to do was call Diane and let her know I was doing good. Or at least lie about being okay. I knew that was the right thing to do but something stopped me every time I tried to reach for my phone.

My hands got the shakes, my eyesight became all fuzzy and my mouth went numb. I was in no condition to talk over the phone with anyone listening on the other side of the line. So I sat and reluctantly accepted whatever disabled me and made me unable to communicate with the girl I loved and banged my head a few times against one of the dirty walls.

I could feel Diane sitting far away in a corner of the house by the phone and thinking about calling me too. I could feel her catching the same thing as me, the same despicable virus that prevented her from reaching out to me in spite of her wanting to. I could feel her tormented by the thought of knowing how I was doing.

I got up and paced the room nervously. Was it the blues? The sad, sad blues that hit me? Had I caught something from smelling the Parisian air or eating in a Parisian neighborhood? The walls were closing again on me, this time shrinking me and the entire house down and reducing everything to a speck of dust flicked into the tranquil waters of the Seine river.

What a way to go! What a way to bow out! What a way to blow away from the world in a shameful reverence dance and be swallowed by impressionable art or modern architectures that donned these grounds.

I looked over at the clock. 7:00 p.m. Fuck.

Tomorrow I will call my publisher. My book—which had so far been a commodity to me—was increasingly starting to look like a necessity. I was low on cash and could really use the sales right now. Yes, that's what I'll tell my publisher.

After all, some people you had to rehearse your words with. Others, like Diane, were easy to talk to. Tonight though, I couldn't seem to be able to talk to anyone about anything.

10

SHE FLICKED HER HAIR, bit her lower lip and swallowed me with her big brown eyes. She walked around the apartment in her black lacey lingerie and her feet left stamps all over the wooden floor.

She passed by the closet two or three times and sprayed a bit of her favorite perfume on herself. She knew it was my favorite perfume too. She rubbed it on her elbows and wrists and neck and body.

I finally caved and got up and started chasing her around the house. We ended up where we usually did: in bed. Though the bedroom of this small house was also the dining room (and kitchen, and living area), the moment we sprung our bodies on the bed was the moment we entered a sanctuary. A lair of our own. This would be confirmed to me whenever she whispered, 'We're safe here. Nobody can harm us now.'

It was evident to me there was a rift between our space-time continuum and that of the rest of mankind. Our time was different—we had more say, more control on it. We could make it as slow or as fast as we pleased, distort it as much as we desired, play with it and make it exciting or boring or simply fuck around and fiddle with it until we got tired.

Diane took control of my hands. She felt my arms, touched my protruding shoulder blades and started guiding me through her body. Tenderly, she walked me through the uncharted areas I knew few men had explored before me: her chest, split down the middle perfectly, her elegant breath feeding it with raw sensuality, her hips firm like ripe glorious fruit, her abdomen contracting slowly as if not to disrupt my movement.

I started by caressing her, I started by imprinting my fingers all over her. Whatever I could touch or grab or hold from her body I did. I was selfish with it the way she wanted me to be. Her stare accompanied me up and down, approving every time I touched or licked a part of her.

The moans that came out of her were sweet music to me. Sweet steamy hot-shower firecracker music that thrilled and enthralled me. My soul was enchanted with this woman; my love for her like good old aging scotch—better even.

Diane adjusted her head while I kept working her body and changing the music from romantic jazz to classical piano to soft rock and roll…the gods coming and going through the revolving door with our bodies still pinned on the bed, the sheets smelling of our skins. We made slow soft love and I tenderly penetrated her until we both peaked and the world became bearable once again.

She whispered my name in panting tired little breaths, and I called her by hers once to silence all the waters. Then I got up and walked over to the kitchen area, feeling a little more man, a little more divine, and poured her and myself a glass of orange juice.

I waited for the neighbors to be alerted by the ongoing loud music or our screams but they never came by. I wanted them to feast on the artistry this woman and I were creating, to indulge in the beauty and consummation of true love—but then I thought to myself this was not something I wanted to share with them or anybody else, this was not something I wanted to expose to the world or have robbed and taken away from me. Having Diane in my life was like having the sun; and being deprived of her presence was like a rolling thunder preparing for an incoming meteorite that would come down with unimaginable force on me and shoot my body out of this earth and blast it wide into empty space.

Sometimes I thought about how she moved me, how she made tears appear in my empty eyeballs—tears that hadn't known their way up there for more than 20 years now—but seemed to find their path when I stared at her or clasped her hand in mine or rubbed my foot against her ankle when we were sitting together. It was that kind of emotion that made me feel and accept being human for a while. Diane knew it just like she knew my extreme distaste toward mankind in general and my unflinching will to be of the least benefit to their kind as I could be. She gave me a tough time about it sometimes and told me there was more to them than I thought, but I told her she couldn't take away my opinion.

'Look at us,' she said, smiling like an innocent child.

'Yeah, what about us?'

'Look how happy we are.'

'Yeah.'

'People can do that. People can make each other happy.'

'Not all people...'

She then pulled her legs together and crossed them, placing her hands on mine and closing them. 'I promised myself not to fall in love. Yet here I am with you.'

'Yeah.'

'Love isn't real, is it?'

'I don't think so.'

'I mean, what we're feeling now, what we feel, it's just from the moment, right?'

'Maybe.'

'Can you not be so passive?'

'I'm not sure love isn't real. It might and it might not be.'

'Now you're being indecisive.'

'Baby, give me your hand.' She extended it. 'Do you feel this?'

'Yes.'

'What does it feel like?'

'Electricity.'

'That's all we need to know. The current that's flowing between us is all that matters. As long as it's not cut, there's a good chance love is something real.'

I woke up in darkness. In a new bed, sleeping on an unfamiliar mattress. The bed squeaked every time I took a deep breath. I had what looked like permanent marks on my chest from sweating.

I turned around to figure out what time it was but there wasn't a single clock in the house. My phone battery was dead and it didn't want to wake up.

I decided it was the middle of the night. Diane was still out there, sleeping in her bed. Our bed. Our sanctuary of love.

I laid on my back again on the half-broken mattress bed. I closed my hands together and felt nothing.

No current. No electricity.

No love.

Just the barking of a mad dog like a shout in the sad dark.

54

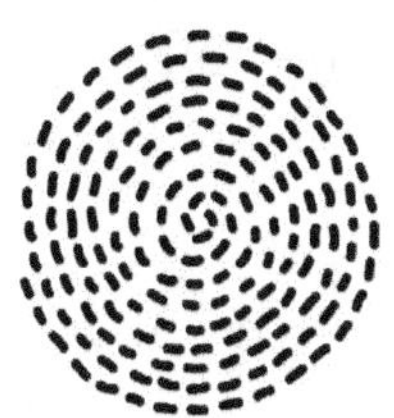

11

MY PUBLISHER WAS A keen man. He knew how to bide his time well and when to act. This helped him especially in dealing with difficult people like me. He was cunning and intelligent, even if I didn't really like to admit it.

I phoned him earlier today but he didn't pick up. So I decided to scout the area nearby in the hopes of befriending a new liquor store owner or coffee shop caretaker and procure myself my necessary supply of booze and caffeine.

With the whole house-hopping thing going, my body intake was low and began to crave both. I started to wallow and yawn like a moron, walk up and down my little dirty house like a modern-day nitwit, and drink water (the only thing available to me) and pee in excess. I started the day like a nincompoop and needed some grounding.

Luckily, my phone came back to life after a few hours of charging and I had a few missed calls from Diane. I decided I needed to talk to her—but not now. Not like this, feeling weary and groggy and weak. She was never going to have the loser she let go of so I decided to become a winner. A serial winner. If saying it long enough made it true, I was ready to keep repeating it all day.

I went down to the streets and saw some of Paris's most exciting pillars flashing above me. They were buildings that touched the sky and made it seem like I was walking inside a doll house. Everything outside my reach seemed out of proportion, and the things I had to do with only shrunk further in size.

I gained some hope when my eyes caught a liquor store. I went inside and introduced myself with a fake name (that way I was sure they wouldn't remember me) and purchased a flask of Label 5.

That would get me through part of the day at least. The liquor man had a happy smile on his face while selling me the booze, as did the rest of the customers in that small shop. Everyone around seemed trigger happy it made me question my own sanity and misery. Was it really that easy to just let things be and be happy? To just wake up every morning and fuck off every worry scratching your fibers and just let it go?

I couldn't see it. I went to a park nearby and decided to put my drinking talents on display. It was true that I wasn't dependent on alcohol, that I didn't need it to survive. But there was something to put on for show every time my brain reached for the bottle and started to consume from it. There was poetry in the slow, faltering self-destruction of a man that could be demonstrated and witnessed by the measured drinking of a small bottle of concentrated whiskey. It was one of the few things that reminded me how destructible I was, just like war did.

After some time drinking I could feel my brain becoming crippled and going numb. I was sitting under a tree and decided

I'd shut off there. I didn't know how long I was out for before my phone began vibrating in my right pocket.

'Yeah?'

'John? Am I disturbing you?'

It was the freaking publisher.

'Nah, nah.'

'How are you?'

'Okay.'

'Your voice seems a little tired.'

'I just woke up.'

'Ah…well then this will shake you up real good! It's done!'

'What's done?'

'The book! Your book! It's done! I received the final version for the cover and sent the whole thing for print last week! And now I'm talking to you while holding the first paperback in my hands! We're going to start making money out of this!'

'That's great.'

'I wanted to call you and personally give you the news head-on. Prepare yourself John, you're going to become a bestselling millionaire of an author!'

'Yeah.'

I hung up. He was still rejoicing or even crying on the other side of the line. His words stuck on me. BESTSELLING MILLIONAIRE AUTHOR. I didn't feel like a soon-to-be millionaire.

Maybe it was my body still reacting to the big news. Maybe it was the realization it was finally becoming real. Maybe a part of me stopped caring after losing other things. In any case, if there was going to be some celebration about all this, I needed to be with the person that believed in it more than me: Diane.

She foresaw it all from the time this book was still a naked, title-less, cover-less mass of paper. Fleeting thoughts, I used to refer to it. But for someone to always push for those inquisitions and postulations and want to see them turned into reality and truth, that was her force alone.

I got up and dragged myself across the park, holding onto anything until I could find my rhythm and walk straight again. I had to go see Diane. She would be at work now, but there was nothing I could think of doing other than waiting for her in front of her door.

On my way out of the park, an officer blew his whistle and halted me for crossing a pedestrian street light, a bum stopped me to give me money because I looked worse off than him, but I wouldn't be stopped. I had one objective: get to that train station and take the train to Diane.

I was surprised at my own will and the strength it incurred in me. It did a good job at fending off the nasty alcohol bubbling in me and dissolving my insides. But I was relentless. If anything was worth doing in this life, it had to be done by force and resistance. The last thing I could imagine was submitting and lying on the gravel floor like an old rug. That was not a mark of a proud author—or a soon-to-be one.

The deathly air of another cold day pierced through me as well, but with all my defenses up and alert, there was no chance the sickly weather could get to me. I passed by and scoffed at people coughing and wiping their red nasals with infernal wipes and tissues and made it to my destination. For a minute I got a bad scare because I couldn't find my ticket and thought I left it home. It turned out I had just misplaced it in my oversized raincoat.

Arriving on the boarding platform, I observed the other passengers waiting next to me: people of all shapes and kinds. What were they thinking? Were they all going back to a lover? Were they all feeling defeated and deflated? Were they all on a mission for greatness, fame, validation?

The sound of the incoming train startled me. It gave me little chills in my spine. Kind of like the ones every boy felt on a first date with a girl he really liked.

I boarded without looking back. I was in no hurry to get back. There was nothing waiting for me here worth the rush. Up ahead though was a clearer sky, a better weather, a healthier oxygen waiting to be breathed.

Most importantly, there was the semblance of any kind of future I could possibly imagine for myself.

12

Diane was walking towards me with a Gitanes smoke in her mouth. She was puffing out grey circles that made little holes in the clouds.

'That's a nice trick,' I told her.

'What are you doing here?'

'I just want to talk.'

'I don't want to talk to you.'

I beat her to the knob and screened the door for her.

'What do you want, John?' she said.

'I told you, I just want to talk. Can I come in?'

'It looks like you've already forced yourself halfway in.'

She forced herself on the door and pushed her keys in. 'Come on in,' she said.

She took off her jacket and threw her bag on the floor. 'I'm tired,' she said. I recognized right there the mental drain affecting her body. Diane's emotions were a powerful engine that dictated a large portion of her functionality—as long as they were intact.

Any emotional toll on her made her shut down completely and resign her body and mind to extensive fatigue.

'I'll make us coffee,' I said.

'I don't want coffee,' she said, lying on the bed. 'Tell me what you want.'

'I want to talk about us.'

'Really? About us? You wouldn't even return my calls and you're here to talk about us?'

'Yeah.'

'I don't think there's anything to talk about. Do you know how many times I called you?'

'A lot.'

'Do you know how many times? How many times?'

'I don't know.'

'Say a fucking number!'

'20.'

'Asshole!'

She sat straight. 'I want you to leave me alone.'

'It's out, Diane. It's out.'

'What's out?'

'My book…it's been published. I talked to the publisher and they're releasing it. We made it.'

'Well woo-hoo! Fucking congratulations to you! Do you think I fucking care about you or your book after the way you treated me? After the way you left?'

'You were the one that kicked me out.'

'And you left!'

Diane got up and lit another smoke.

'You know what John? Congratulations on your book. It's been a long time coming. I know how much you've put into it.

You deserve it. But you don't fucking deserve me. So get out of my house.'

'Diane…'

'I have nothing to say to you anymore. Please leave.'

'Listen to me…'

'PLEASE. LEAVE. BEFORE I MAKE YOU.'

'You're not listening to me.'

'LEAVE NOW!'

I got up and walked out. It was a familiar scene, a déjà-vu that replayed in my head. Funny how as I was leaving time was slowly freezing as if to give me a chance to fix my mistake. But it was all the same. I had reached a buggy impasse with Diane: one that no longer held together on communication and conversation but seizing each other up until one of us backed into a corner. This time I was the loser who stumbled in the confrontation and missed the finish line. I had run out of breath in uncharacteristic fashion, something I didn't recognize in myself.

It bugged me to walk out on Diane again. It bugged me to not be able to fix my mistake, to fix us. I needed her, I wanted her, I couldn't be with her. Did it mean love failed? Or was it never meant for us from the start? I was in the streets again, streets I walked so much coming back and forth into this house. I saw my trips lining up in front of my eyes: walks to the supermarket, to the park, to the museum, to the library, to the bad sushi place at the corner. I ingrained part of myself here, I planted memories and footsteps and breaths and drops of sweat and tears. Didn't any of those mean anything? Didn't the kisses and the music and the light dancing and the late-night cuddles give me any leverage? No.

Because love wasn't measured by steps or numbers or acts. There was a mystique to it I hadn't fully caught yet, a trade I hadn't gotten the grips of. It was too complicated for me and stretched beyond my reasoning.

I boarded the train back home still thinking about my last exchange with Diane. The way I stood there stiff like a tree branch while she poured herself in a small coffee cup in front of me and drank it in a gulp. While she berated me all I could do was stare at her. I wasn't the man she wanted. Hell, I wasn't even the man I wanted. Now it was all gone, in a flash, like a mudslide in the rain, like the last layer of grease in an unclogged sink.

I got off the train and walked from the station to the house. A package was sitting in front of my doorstep. It was a big brown carton. I shook it and tore it open and found a pile of bubble wrap. There was a note inside inscribed with the following:

'Here's the first step to success. Enjoy it after the hard work. Yours.'

The signature was unmistakably that of my publisher. He had sent me my 'share' of the first batch of published books. Since modern publishing could never estimate the success of a newly-released book, especially with readership varying at uncertain levels, my guy decided to play it safe and started out with a few prints. This meant that I, the author of the book, was the proud recipient of ONE copy of my book. One print copy of a year's worth of work. It wasn't a fair deal, but most things in life weren't.

I touched the book in my hand and felt the cover, the binding, the paper. I opened it and sniffed the pages looking for that elusive paper book smell. It was there. I flipped the pages and saw the words jump from right to left. I read them like I was reading the words of a stranger. Yet here I was, a writer, a published writer, a certified writer. I looked at the sky. It was pale dark, turning black, ordinarily grim. The buildings were shying away, illuminating their floors one by one. The neighbors were walking their dog on the other side of the street and stopping at the fire hydrant by the corner so it could take a leak. All my dreams were coming into fruition in a single moment on a not-so-special night in Paris.

Yet I knew it was my night. The sad reality was that nobody else did. Actually, there was one other person who knew. But given the choice, I thought that person would rather not know me or have anything to do with me at the moment.

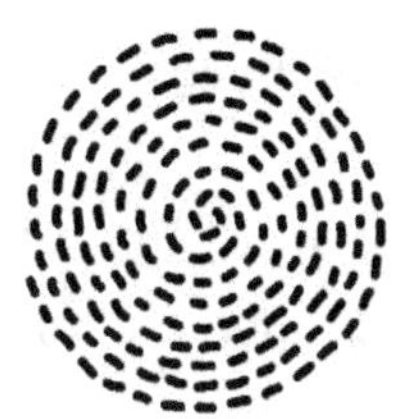

13

I CROSSED TOLSTOÏ SQUARE and made it to the market. With the little money I had left, I intended to stock up on my already-low supply of alcohol and coffee.

I went for the usual suspects: a bottle of Jim and two bottles of Jack. I decided not to go for the coffee beans and bought the little bags of powder caffeine instead just because I was lazy. What the hell, a man deserved at least to drink his coffee in peace.

The store owner gave me a little friendly smile at the checkout. I could never remember his name but I knew he remembered mine. His eyebrows got a little too excited every time he ran one of my alcohol bottles on the machine and he gave me dirty little looks. I didn't know what any of it meant.

I took out whatever money was left in my pocket and paid. The store man carefully placed the bills and loose change in front of me and started adding them up to make sure the payment was good. I sometimes worried about people being too conscious about things like money. They could use a little more chaos brought into their lives, a little anarchy that would blow up all payment systems into large clouds of smoke too toxic to even breathe.

I was unconscious when it came to money. Of course, that had its flaws too but it strangely made me feel loose and free instead of being grounded all the time. Yes, money grounded people. In fact, it made them crawl like little weak creatures under the hateful sun. The store man was like that. The fish market man was like that. The bar man down the corner was like that.

I bagged my stuff (I had to pay for the bag as well) and was on my way again. This time I felt much more powerful coming out of the store than coming empty-handed. Outside I ran into Antoine and he stopped me to say hello.

Antoine was a middle-aged family man. He had a nice wife and 3 children, all out of college and into the working world. He was also very wealthy. I knew this because he was involved with several charitable organizations and they all solicited him for financial purposes.

'John, my good man! It's good to see you!' he said.

'It's good to see you too.'

'What's this I hear? You're a published writer now?'

'Where did you hear that?'

'News travels fast, my boy! HO HO, I remember when we sat at that old café in Paris not long ago and you told me your name was going to appear in every bookstore in France one day!'

'I believe I said, in every bookstore in the world…'

'HA HA, there's that sense of humor I like! So tell me, where can I get my hands on that book of yours?'

'Well, it's being offloaded to bookstores as we speak.'

'You mean distributed?'

'That's what I said.'

'Well then, how much time would you estimate before it appears in France?'

'I would give it a week.'

'But don't you have any copies you could spare? You are the writer after all!'

'Actually, I received a single print. No more than that.'

'That's absurd! But you are the writer after all!?'

'Yeah, well, I guess that's why writers die poor. They never live long enough to walk in their own light.'

'Very well then. I shall wait for the book to be available locally. I look forward to reading it—erm, you!'

'You could always go online and order it…'

'Come on John, you know these things aren't made for someone like me! I don't trust them!'

'Yeah, neither do I.'

Back at the apartment, I took off all my clothes and tried to empty my pockets. There was no money left in them. I had a small apartment with a basket full of dirty clothes, a bag of coffee and alcohol from the store, one copy of my recently published book and no money.

I opened my window. There were kids playing in the street. They were running around and pulling at each other's hairs. I remembered when I was a kid—I was too skinny to rough it up with the other boys, too awkward to kick a football and too slow to play tag or chase around others. The only game I was good at was hide and seek. Mainly because I was good at hiding. I was pretty good at picking out spots no one would think of looking in. And hiding always gave me my own space away from others. It made me feel a bit different—like I didn't need to be part of a crowd to stand out.

Today I didn't feel like part of the crowd either. It was like they were all looking in one direction and I was looking in another. But what were they so focused on? What was so important they had to look at it all together? Maybe Diane was right. Maybe my publisher was right. Maybe I was just a sad selfish man who drank a lot and made too much of his writing.

I picked up the phone and tried calling Diane.

BEEP. BEEP. BEEP. No answer. BOOP.

Re-dial.

BEEP. BEEP. BEEP.

BOOP.

I dropped the phone on the bed and did the next best thing: drink. The smell of alcohol was like an aroma filling the room. It even got the little insects living in the corners of the house excited and made them pop out of their holes. The assholes— they weren't having any of my drink.

Here's to me, the latest in a breed of demented madmen who swore loyalty to the word. And now that I had upheld my end of the bargain I was ready to receive my dues. The tours, the signings, the conferences, the college readings, maybe a movie credit even. It could all happen and I could see it happening. The problem was it wasn't happening fast enough.

I'd outgrown Paris. I'd outgrown this city and these people. I was already thinking about the next move, about destinations, destinations, destinations. The moving man who left a few words wherever he went. That was my only trace.

While injecting more booze into my body I was thinking about the pillars of life. How many were there: Four? Five? Ten?

And how many of them did we need to make it a good life? It didn't matter anyway, now. Now, everything was in tatters. Everything was scattered like marbles on the floor beneath me. Marbles of human faces, faces that I knew. Marbles of stone and steel and jade and aqua. Marbles of double wood and honey.

Let me lie down a bit here. Let me give way to tomorrow. Maybe things got so complicated they ended up loosening a bit. It was Hemingway who said we find escape in sleep when life tends to fall apart.

I decided to put my faith in Hemingway. And sleep, sleep, sleep the early night away…

14

ALRIGHT. OKAY. SO WAKING up every day with the filth of alcohol in my mouth and almost no money, I decided it was time to go look for a job. Just something to help me get by until my book sales royalties started kicking in.

The last thing I wanted now was the new landlady on my back threatening to kick me out. I had already enough enemies as is and the more I could cut down on them, the better it was for me I figured.

I got my cleanest shirt (the cleanest of 3) and started hunting down possible employers. I chose to work in fields where I thought I could pose best as a serious candidate—sales and marketing.

Turns out I didn't.

In an era where the consensus was heading towards simplifying and speeding, the interview process was still pretty damn long. I had to wait in line for nearly every position I applied for— and only to meet a single person in a suit (generally cleaner and shinier than my clothes) who would give me an appointment for another interview.

It was common practice everywhere, especially in France. The French were unforgiving, punctual and irritatingly meticulous— or maybe that was just how you became once you'd set foot in the corporate world. In any case, I could tell they were all very much different from me. They used corporate terms like multidisciplinary, overtime, efficiency, outlet. Their vocabulary was contaminated with a bunch of them, most of which I had to make an effort to forget. They emphasized on honesty (and required it from all candidates), yet one of the employers fell into a deep state of shock and incredulity when he asked about my professional experience and I answered him frankly that I was a writer. Times had shifted alright. Artists were scorned and frowned upon and deemed immediately not good enough or even out of their depths in the corporate world. Since when was writing books no longer good enough? I was a published author, a soon-to-be in-demand name, a commodity on the market and I was being treated like any other beggar on the streets.

Actually, the beggars somehow had more decency than me. Everywhere I walked I watched them come up to people and ask for money. There was no more shame in begging—the shame had turned on the people who refused to 'help' them. They guilted themselves with it and hid their heads in their hands while shying away from the determined beggars.

I wish I could be a beggar. I wish I had that kind of courage. But I didn't. I was a selfish little man who wanted a taste of the sun without having to stand in the sunlight. That was why writing was good to me: it allowed me to demonstrate myself without asking too much from me. It took whatever I had and turned it into something interesting. I didn't have to be special or have some kind of skill or be able at anything for it to just transform me into something higher, a magnified version of my little self that was fitting enough to reserve a small place in the world. That was it. Writing gave me a spot on the turf of the world.

I talked to employees about my ability to stay up hours in front of a computer and type until my fingers bled. But even that wasn't enough to impress them. They explained they were looking for a different set of computer skills—a skillset I didn't really have. I was never good with the computer and never interested in becoming any better. I thought of it the same way I thought of a car: I needn't know much about it as long as I understood its general functionality and was able to put it to use. As a man and a writer, that was all I really needed.

In truth I was never really eager to get a job. And I think they sensed it. I think something in me gave me away every time I sat in that chair to get interviewed. I just didn't know what it was.

My publisher had been calling me frantically for the past 3 days to check up on me. He was worried I would already be on the top of the highest pillar thanks to my book release. I told him I was still floundering in a kiddy pool and splashing in every direction.

'Aren't you happy?' he asked me annoyingly.

'Happy? Why would I be happy? The book's not even available in all the bookstores and it's been almost a month since the release was announced!'

'it was released last week…'

'Don't give me that.'

'Look, John, it's a process. These things take time. This is your first major writing breakthrough. And no matter how much the real world appreciates published writers, there's a process to be respected. There's no other way.'

'Well your process is coming out of my time! I've already turned away several buyers! Not to mention I still live in a dunghole on my own.'

'Weren't you living with your girlfriend?'

'Not anymore.'

'John, I'm concerned about you. Is there something I need to know?'

'No. just make sure they hurry up with the books. People are starting to get impatient here.'

◡

A moth in the park
It's 5.00 pm
Still no luck
Out in the cold
The apartment dreary
Teenage boys cutting in front of me
To do their laundry
And smoke hash
On the dryer
I have a supermarket list
But no money
My stomach is growling
But I can't think about food

Baby, it's cold
But I can see a moth
A little orb of yellow light

Floating in the air
From one lamp post
To another

I observe it
From the park bench
The cold wood
Freezing my prancing ass
I remember how much you like
Moths
How highly you speak of them
Because they are attracted by the light
Just like you
You say you would like to be reborn
As one
Now that I watch it
Now that I pay close attention
To this moth
I think
They are not bad
After all
Hehe
Little flashing creatures of the night
Little candles floating until first light

Candles
Like the candle set you always have
On your dining table
Vanilla-scented
That's another thing

You really like
Candles—bringing together
Sight and smell
Reconciling the senses
I admire your senses
Your sensuality
Your erotic naked raw vulnerability
Dripping emotion
Dripping on the wet shower floor
All the way to the bedroom…

I think that
All in all
I would like to be
A moth
Tonight;

That wouldn't be
Such
A terrible
Thing.

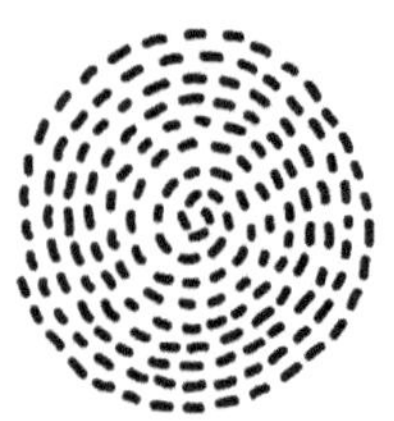

15

My father was an accountant. I never really knew what his job involved when I was younger except that he worked long hours and came back home late at night. That's all I got to see from it as a kid. My mother would sometimes get upset with him for not spending enough time with us and they would fight over it, too.

But my father was an honorable man. He always tried to do the right thing and be there for his family. He took pride in his work; he took pride in the hours he put and in being an accountant.

I remembered being proud of him in my own special way. Not the kind of pride that would end in me talking him up to my school friends or wanting to become an accountant too. But the kind of pride that made me always look high up at him with respect. That was my own secret way.

My father left this world with a smile on his face. I remember him on his deathbed—lying there, not giving a fuck about dying and disappearing into thin space. I'm sure he would've still been the greatest accountant had he decided to take up work on his hospital bed with a half-functioning heart. Although he never got me to believe in accounting, my father did get me to believe in things.

He got me believing that no job is mediocre or banal. That every effort you put in any job counts. 'Always respect the profession you're in,' he used to tell me. 'It'll be your source of income and life. The more you give it, the more it gives back. Just like a garden.'

I liked the idea of the garden. I liked the idea of harvesting something you worked hard for. And the more I thought of it, the farther away I found it from writing. It didn't correlate well with the craft and my brain suddenly had a hard time figuring out why I chose to become a writer.

Writing had its own methods. It was an entirely different process from any other job or labor or work. The outcome was never directly proportional to the amount of time or effort you put into it. Instead, it came in increments. Varying increments at varying intervals of time. Sometimes it peaked quite early. Sometimes it dried up for years before picking up again. Sometimes it never gave back and you spent a lifetime waiting for it to do so.

I felt cheap. I felt robbed by writing. It was a ploy, a silly device that lured wishful fools into it and sucked their lives away. I tended to think it, and any other art form in general, were just mechanisms put in place by governments and political people to eliminate the weak and naïve. A sort of trimming of the population. Well I was it. I was part of the batch. I was one of the hopeful morons who had been snared up by that net and was left floundering for dead in it.

I'd given writing everything: my time, my effort, my life. Now as I waited for it to give back, I felt it restraining its grip and pulling away from me. I tried to nudge it but it wouldn't bulge. It was a stubborn bitch.

The game of writing wasn't fair. You could be an honorable man and lose. You could be a scumbag and lose. I wasn't sure which one I was but I was definitely in the 'loser' section.

That pissed me off. It got me to think about some writers: Fante, Kerouac, Ginsberg, Burroughs, Dostoevsky. And some others, more contemporary and commercialized writers I won't bother mentioning. I thought about those guys, I thought hard about their words - how they ranged from great to mediocre. The greats, the past greats were of course untouchable. But the new guys—the pretenders—were far less impressive and borderline disappointing. In plain text, they were simply shit. A big pile of it. How they gathered a following of sheep was both shocking and troubling to me.

I thought about those guys, then I thought about myself and my kind of writing, and I said, surely, I can do better than that. I can write better than them. Not like the greats of course but at least better than the shits. I knew that out of tact and downright simple logic. I had different motives, different ambitions to fulfill through my writing. I never wrote for the radio interviews or then bus-banner commercials or the billboard posters or the internet ads. I wrote to get some sort of truth out, to make it heard by as many people as possible. I thought that if one person ever picked up one of my books and read my stuff…then that person can become two. Four. Sixteen. A hundred.

But it didn't have to be any fixed or imaginable number. Just some number of people I would know my words were getting through. That would be enough to help me sleep at night (I hadn't been getting much lately).

But it was hard to hold on to such a noble cause and be a writer all the same. It was hard to stick to the word form in a world of scripts and tv screens, of lights, cameras and movies. It was hard to resist jumping ship, especially somewhere where the opportunities were there. I could very well be scooped up by some hot-shot agent right here in the middle of Paris and negotiate a movie script the next day. Bukowski did it. Fante did it. They played in that courtyard and the bucks started rolling in. Soon writing became ephemeral. Just a little whim or whimsical *passe-temps*.

For me it was still solid. I couldn't see the end of this whole book release mess, but I had that gut feeling that was telling me it was there. And each time I found myself doubting the gut pressed on. And on and on and on. It pressed down hard on my thighs and made my legs shake. I had to drink to numb the pain and forget about it. Luckily I had the Jack and the Johnny and the Jim and they all had my back. I had to stay healthy (or at least mortal) if I were to witness the book come to life and ejaculate words in people's hands.

I checked my phone. No calls from the publisher. None from Diane. I let my mind wonder about her and what she had been up to. It's been a long time since I hadn't smelled her—I believed it was Bukowski who advocated solitude. Or was it John Fante who preached it for the writer?

Not for me. I felt I needed someone more than ever now, especially with the book falling out by the day. I had to have someone or be with someone who would reassure me it would all be okay. Writing couldn't provide me with that kind of security and assurance. It had put me in that mess and left me out in the cold.

Maybe my father was right. He never discouraged me to write but to be fair he never advocated it either. I'd like to believe that in another life, he had given it a fair shot too and switched careers when he saw the end of it. I liked to believe things worked out for him that way in the end.

I went to the fridge and opened a new bottle of Jack. I wanted to believe things would work out for me as well.

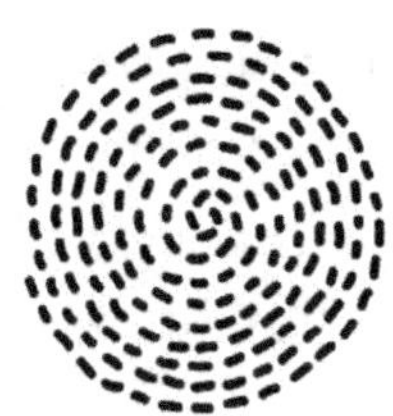

16

I RECEIVED A TEXT message and a letter from the electricity company saying I should report my consumption (which was indexed in small numbers on the meter in my apartment) so that they could bill me.

I slouched into the apartment half-drunk. I had previously gathered my energy and invested it in a half-pint of Black Label in the park. I also tried starting up on a new read—a contemporary novel—but it didn't speak to me and I quickly gave it up after the first few pages.

Reading was becoming a bore. And by reading I meant the lack of reading material. Good reading material. It was hard to find something that touched you like the great novels—especially when you were low on budget.

Well I was on no budget. I had skimmed my badly-ironed jeans once more and scraped it for pennies or wriggled paper money and come up short again. At this point I realized making money in order to survive should be my main concern ahead of my next read.

Anyhow, I examined the right wall of my apartment and was successful in locating my electric meter. The rectangular thing was covered in dust almost entirely, and I had to wipe off a few layers before I was able to clearly read the screen. I read the numbers registered once in my mind, then aloud to make sure I had them correctly.

I read up the number of the electrical company marked at the bottom of the letter. I dialed it and waited on the line.

The first voice that greeted me was an answering machine. Before my mind could catch up with the first sentence, I was flooded with a series of options, each conveniently accompanied by its corresponding keypress. Finally after the instructions ran out, I was asked to wait until I was transferred to a human correspondent. I was caller number 11 in the queue.

I must've waited a good 20 mins before I got any sign of contact on the other end. YOU ARE NUMBER 10 IN THE QUEUE, the machine declared.

YOU ARE NUMBER 9 IN THE QUEUE, it gleefully repeated.

By the time it counted down to number 5, I felt it was mocking me.

By that time, my body was giving me signs it needed alcohol. My hands were sweaty, they started shivering, my legs were shaking uncontrollably. I needed a drink. I was angry at the waiting queue, I was angry at the electricity company, I was angry I didn't have any money, I was angry I didn't have a good book to read.

I needed a drink. I could feel the sweat forming on my forehead, the air around me suddenly turning crisp and raw, my paperless mouth running dry. I tried to look around the apartment to get away from my agitation, but I stumbled on dust balls and breadcrumb remains (now hardened) trailing on the wood board floor.

As I flailed around helplessly in the room the machine was doing its best to delay any form of response I would get. The line would go silent, only to occasionally come back to life to remind me I had moved up one spot in the waiting queue. Were all these people mad? Were all of them in need to dial in their numbers at the exact same time? I tended to forget I was not alone in the world, but I operated on a different frequency from the rest that it was hard for me to accept it whenever I converged towards them.

I was a sheep. Running after companies to declare my consumptions, paying bills, buying verified stamps online to latch onto administrative paperwork that were doomed to get banished to a registry and be forgotten forever. I had been institutionalized. I thought it was funny how things like that stretched on, but we never caught up to them until after it was too late.

Finally as my body grew weak and weary and my kneecaps almost busted from the rest of me and I lost the support of my legs, I fell to my knees, one hand on the floor and the other desperately grabbing the phone and holding it to my ear—still hoping someone would answer me and relieve me of my agony. The sweat was dripping from my shoulders and arms and face, covering my shirt in large wet stains and forming small puddles on the floor. I thought I was going to die. I thought about my legacy. About the people. About how they would remember me. They would write on my obituary: MAD WRITER. COULDN'T WRITE PAST HIS FIRST AND ONLY PUBLISHED BOOK. DIED OF WAITING ON LIFE AND TALENT.

It would be classless but true. In the space of a short amount of time I had seen myself shrink from a soon-to-be-prodigy of the literary world into an abysmal loser. A downright bum. At first I thought I was fulfilling some unspoken prophecy—the one some of us tended to buy into when we read the great writers. The starving writers. The poor writers. The mad writers. But we weren't like them—we couldn't be. The world was mad enough to drive anyone insane, we didn't need literature for that. But we still needed it for truth—we were desperately short in that area. And today, I couldn't write for truth. I couldn't write worth a damn and I knew it. I could barely stick it to the end of this call.

Just as my body entered its final surrender and I was about to cave, a voice broke in from the other side of the line and startled me. It was a human voice, I was sure. But it spoke in a more mechanical way than the answering machine.

'Hello, this is Michelle speaking. How may I help you?'

'Yes, hello. First of all, let me start by stating how wonderful your answering machine is! It really takes the cake in terms of customer service! The thing overwhelms clients with more options than they would ever need and overloads their brains before they even get the chance to state the intention of their call. Brilliant stuff!'

'Sir, how may I help you?'

'I would like to report my consumption index.'

'Just a moment sir, the line is cutting. Are you in an open space?'

'I am in my apartment.'

'There seems to be quite a lot of echo. It is noisy and I can't understand you well. Is it possible for you to move or change your location sir?'

'I can't do that.'

'Sir, I'm unable to hear you properly.'

'I said I can't move.'

'What's your request sir?'

'I would like to communicate my consumption index.'

'Very well, sir. Just a moment to load up the database and look up your file. I'll have to ask you to kindly wait on-line with me.'

'Ok.'

'In the meantime, may I have your name sir? It will make the search easier for me.'

'John Kaliba.'

'Is that with a C or a K sir?'

'It's a K.'

'One moment please, sir. I'm going to have to ask you to stay on the line with me…'

'Good news, sir. I was able to identify your profile. Now, you are located on Tolstoï square, correct?'

'Correct.'

'…in a 17,67 square meter apartment. Furnished and equipped with a fridge and a built-in heater.'

'The heater is shared with the other apartments. It has a central distributor.'

'Yes, I can see that sir. Now, this will be your first electrical bill since moving in, correct?'

'Correct.'

'Very well. Please provide me with your index so we can charge your consumption.'

'660.'

'660 since the start of the month. Correct, sir?'

'Correct.'

'Very well. One moment. I will add the information to the file. If you'll just stay on the line with me…'

'Okay.'

'I'm sorry sir. I'm having trouble saving your information. It seems there is a system malfunction.'

'Can you please try again?'

'Sir, the system isn't responding. This kind of bug isn't uncommon and generally takes time to get the system back up and running. You'll have to call again in 2 days.'

'What? That can't be right.'

'I apologize for the inconvenience sir. Please call us in two days and report your consumption.'

'But I just gave you my index. Can't you just note it down on a piece of paper and enter it later in the system?'

'I'm afraid it doesn't work like that sir. You'll have to call again in two days.'

'But I waited. I was put on hold. I was caller number 11. I listened to your annoying hold music for 25 goddamn minutes!'

'Sir, please call again in 2 days.'

'I don't understand this. I'm a good citizen. I pay my bills. I don't litter on the street or in the park. I don't want to be cut off my electricity because of your stupid system!'

'Sir, please. There's really nothing I can do.'

'BULLSHIT!'

'Is there anything else I can do for you sir?'

'GO FUCK YOURSELF.'

17

DIANE WAS ON MY mind. Now everything seemed to remind me of her: the trees outside made me think of her free-flowing hair in the wind, her yellow summer dress, her white Adidas shoes with pink stripes on the sides.

I wanted to see her again. The way our last encounter fell out left a kind of poison in me. It was intoxicating my insides and making my breathing more difficult.

I walked outside under a rare sunlight. Trees and flowers I had seen for the first time and couldn't name were being moved by the wind and bathed in light solar rays. It was a beautiful day. A beautiful life.

But everything felt dark for me. The outside felt like the crippled insides of my small apartment, the air as suffocating and intoxicating. I was being offered something I couldn't enjoy or be part of—all because of one person. Missing that person meant forgetting about my book troubles, my money troubles, my reading troubles, my drinking troubles.

Thinking about Diane weakened me but it also gave me a kind of resilience. Her memory had become associated with incompleteness—any kind of life without her felt unfulfilled and lacking.

I decided not to stay beat. Not to kick myself down and stay on the curb. I decided to try again with her.

But her voice came back to me and I remembered words she spoke during our last fight. She mentioned I was heading down a dark path, a path I couldn't see, a path of nothingness. She said, you're becoming a lazy shit, a fucktard who thinks he's a know-it-all or finally got it made when he hasn't. You're running towards your doom, and you can't brake or stop or leverage it. You're becoming a good-for-nothing.

I resented that. I contested her words with utter disgust running through my face. First I thought it was directed at her and her reproach, but now I'm starting to think it was more about me and the image I was fading into. No matter what I told Diane, I felt I was losing in this particular argument. Nothing I said appeared to convince her or win her back. I couldn't blame her—I half-believed what I was saying myself. Since the news of the book release, my life had hit a wall and embroiled into a still-stop motion. Now I felt it tumbling downhill and heading for the stop-stop finality.

I tried to concentrate and remember the full flow of words between the two of us. There was a lot of crying, a lot of cursing, a lot of emotion. Blame, reproach, attack. In between, small signs of caring and suppression of feelings. Bubbling of the mind and saturation of the soul.

It then came back to me. The last thing she had said, the final proof as she called it, of my utmost abject state and incompetence, was the fact that I couldn't even muster a single poem out of my mind anymore. I couldn't translate anything on paper. She accused me of not being able to write to save my life, when I once needed to write just to stay alive. I rejected her claims but had nothing to show for it. Which I now realize only made her point stronger.

I wanted to show Diane I wasn't over. I wanted to show her we weren't over. I needed to prove to her there was something left in this walking, drinking, babbling carcass. Something deserving of a chance or worth gambling on.

I decided to sit down and write a poem. I started jotting down an idea I thought was pretty good, but the heavy apartment air got to me. I had to get out. I packed a small bag with a notebook and something to write with, a couple of beers, a chocolate bar and my only copy of my own book. I thought carrying it around and having it under my nose would serve as inspiration to write again.

I still couldn't work my poem idea out fully. I thought a change of scenery was needed. So I hopped (illegally) on a train that dropped me off in one of Paris's unknown, unheard-of neighborhoods. I had stumbled on that neighborhood by mistake a while back and discovered a bookstore in one of its streets. San Francisco books—an ancient bookstore almost as old as Paris itself. They brought in used second-hand books from the States and sold them for cheap. This was interesting because among the stacks of old books you could find rare ones written by the great writers that had gone out of print.

I traced that bookstore the first time I discovered it and made myself a regular, buying all my books from there—when I had money. But I needed a good read and I was short on good books and cash and I thought, hey, why not just head there and poke around the sections a bit? Maybe read a few decent pages or just catch a smell of the old paper.

The store was like a sanctuary. Inside, it was a reverence dance for all the greats that scaled the heights of the highest form of artistry the human soul could offer. Libraries and dictionaries of compiled words shelved into sections labeled in little cardboard. The store keeper was an old grouch who never greeted or smiled at anyone. He was also a book connoisseur, having read everything the bookstore brought in and memorized the placement of each book in the shop.

But after abusing my visits here I could tell he started to faintly recognize me or at least feel some familiarity toward me each time I set foot in the place.

I walked in, not greeting the owner and throwing half an eye at him as usual, and headed straight to the shelves. I skipped past RELIGION, HISTORY, FANTASY, paused for a moment at POETRY, but continued until I reached FICTION. I was looking for a novel, a consistent body of work that would spark me. Unfortunately, poetry wasn't going to cut it this time and I needed something more powerful than a few lines, no matter how true they were.

I searched the line of books, continued outside the shelf in the little corners where some books that hadn't found their place on the shelf had been stacked, and looked in there as well. I gently took out each book, careful not to accidentally rough it up or tear out one of its pages. Some of them were so old the pages were already faltering and almost falling out, so I made sure to treat those with extra care and delicacy. This holy place brought back the sacredness of literature and its immensity to me: I had forgotten how much of a river it was, how reading a few lines could excite and stimulate a person and make words flood endlessly into his soul. I was jumping in place, fireworks went inside my brain, and I didn't feel like drinking.

The keeper was an old impatient man—he didn't like customers who sagged and dragged along the already tight spaces of the bookstore. This made for a lot of clutter, and I witnessed him personally kick out some people for taking too long to look at or pick books. So I had to work fast.

I had almost finished going over every single item in the FICTION section when I came across a rare gem: Dan Fante's *Chump Change*. Fante was a personal favorite of mine, a writer whose works I had been stalking for a while now without success. I had gotten annoyed and given up on any real chance of owning any of his writing.

I held the frail book in my hands and stared at it. I examined the title and read the author's name again to make sure it was the real thing. I opened the book and flipped the pages. They were clean, yellowish paper that smelled more beautiful than anything in the world. No torn pages. One of them was folded near the top, probably from a previous reader who thought it was a better idea than investing in a proper bookmark. Those people irritated me.

I had to have this book. I took it back to the front desk and waited for the old grumpy keeper to show up. He was at the back rearranging a new set of books in the POLITICS section. Those things had caught on in the last few years, probably from all the scandalous stories they contained. Finally the man reclaimed his place at the desk.

'Excuse me,' I said. 'I'd like to buy this.'

'Twenty-two euros and fifty cents,' he barked.

It hit me. I remembered I wasn't carrying any money. I didn't have any money. I was broke. I couldn't afford this book or any other book.

I couldn't believe my luck. I was this close. This close! This close to getting my hands on a work I spent trips to bookstores and libraries looking for and will probably never see again. I knew this was my only chance to buy it or else everything would go to bust.

I tried to appeal to the man's senses and sentimentality in case he had any.

'Pardon me again, it seems I'm a bit short there on the amount.'

'How much you got?' he snarled.

'Actually, I don't have anything on me at the moment.'

'Then you can't buy the book.'

'But sir, can't we reach some sort of agreement here? I really want this book.'

'You need to return the book.'

'Sir, you don't understand, I have to buy this book.'

His face seemed more annoyed now and was squinting at me with rage.

'Why are you trying to buy a book you can't afford? I don't have time for people like you. I'm running a busy place here.'

'But I really need this book! I must have it!'

'You can't have the book. Hand it back and stop wasting my time!'

'What if I promised to come back and pay for it? What if I signed a paper slip or something? Would you at least set it aside for me?'

'Hand me the book and get out of here or I'll make sure it's the last time you enter this place.'

I handed him the book, still latching onto the last inches of it as the old man wrestled it out of my hands.

There was nothing left to do for me but leave. As I turned away and neared the door, something crossed my mind. From the turn of events, I thought why not give it a shot, even if that meant sticking my face in the owner's one more time. I was already half-screwed here as a customer anyway.

'Excuse me,' I said.

'You again! What do you want?'

'I wanted to ask about the availability of a book.'

'Yeah. What book?' he grumbled.

'Actually, it's a new book by a new writer. You probably haven't heard of him.'

'What's his name?' he was starting to get impatient with me.

'Ke-Kaliba…John Kaliba.'

He paused for a minute, as if he was going over things in his head.

'I don't have him,' he said dryly.

I nodded politely.

After exiting the place, I stopped at the corner of the street to take the heat off from my showdown with the store keeper.

Three kids were kicking a football in the street and they were unceremoniously ushered off by incoming food carts. Because I couldn't afford to sit anywhere, I found a small ledge where I would continue to fiddle with my incomplete poem idea. I used my knee for support and pressed the small notepad on it, jotting down line after line.

No good. The next few days saw me pick up the habit of abusing the availability of paper in my notebook and shredding page after page. I was struggling. The writing wasn't coming through. Also, I had almost exhausted my stock of alcohol and sweets and had no plan for supplies. But I was trying to keep focus: every time I thought about something other than the poem my mind wandered into dangerous territories, thinking about rent, food and alcohol, the electricity bill (I hadn't called them back), Diane, my book, Diane.

Things were closing down on me fast and I knew I couldn't resolve it all at once. Matters had simply slipped out of my hands like being out of money or living in a place I couldn't afford or being a semi-alcoholic. The poem was the only thing I found in my hands and the only thing I could impact. Finishing it was the only way that would bring me a step closer back to Diane and show her I was still serious about my writing.

My book was placed next to me on my writing table. I looked at the cover, trying to figure out how it brought me so much joy when I first laid eyes on it. And what for? I couldn't remember.

I let my face sink in my palms and closed down on the world. Drowned in simmering darkness. Things being whispered in the dark, in flashes like burning candle lights that emerged and faded in front of me. Treacherous things. Empowering conversations being repeated in the mirror while brushing my teeth and washing my face every morning. Drunken sorrowful pieces of wisdom laid on the carpet floor next to an empty drink. The word WRITER coming back like a bad chorus. First in syllables, WRI-TER, WR-I-TER, then all at once, then forever.

I got out. I looked at the book again. My book. I picked it up, felt it, examined it, flipped it, put it back down.

I looked for my phone. I had thrown it somewhere in my bag. I emptied the thing and finally found it. I dialed Antoine's number and waited anxiously for the beep.

When his sloth-like voice answered, I asked him if he was still interested in purchasing my book. He said yes and rejoiced. I believed his enthusiasm.

We agreed to meet at 6:00 PM the following day (it was short notice for the same day, and it gave me room to maneuver past the ticket booth at the station where security was much more lax at night than in broad daylight).

I hung up and grabbed the book. I found a good paper bag from the SF bookstore. I dusted it off and put my book in it. It would rest there until tomorrow.

I took my clothes off and crawled into bed. I sat upright and covered myself with the sheets up to my chin. I stared at the paper bag placed on the writing table. I wasn't really sure what I was doing. A lot of hesitation started to make waves in me, like a series of nasty hiccups. I was troubled at the thought of what I was about to commit, what I was about to inflict to myself as a writer. I worried about the book. I worried about it being abused, neglected, forgotten on some shelf along with a hundred, thousand others that were maybe equally important (or unimportant) to their owner.

Some people collected books for the looks. Some thought of them as ornaments, decorations or props for their libraries. The idea infuriated me and I had to fight off the thought of getting up and withdrawing my offer.

Tonight was going to be difficult. Tonight was going to be a trying night. Tonight would be a night I'd spend reflecting, meditating, and occasionally getting up to pour myself a drink. The book stayed in the paper bag, unmoved, and after a few drinks, I stayed under the sheets. Unmoved too.

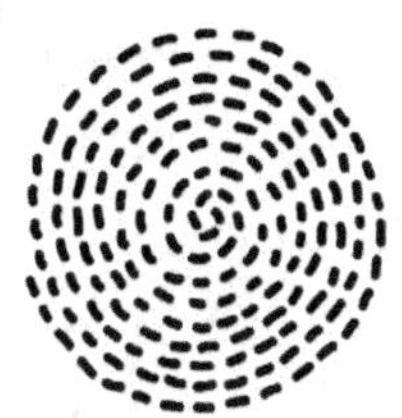

18

ANTOINE WAS WAITING FOR me near a Starbucks in the fifth district. Originally, he had suggested we meet inside a café and even offered to buy me coffee. Normally I would have accepted, but given the circumstances, I preferred not to have this meeting drag on and end it as quickly as possible.

I arrived a bit later than him to the meeting point with my book still in its paper bag. On the way over, I had been thinking about the meaning of this book to me.

When it got published, this book was everything: a pathway to success, wealth and fame. Recognition. Legendary status. It would've been a symbol of my talent and a testimony to scaling the giant mountain that often stands in the way of a writer's path. But since then, it had fallen abysmally from its stature—and my heart with it. Yes, this book contained a part of my soul, my words, my ideals, but it also handicapped me. It froze the hot blood in my veins and turned it ice cold. I didn't need to have the soul of a musician to be an artist but I also didn't need my own book to be given unlimited license to create. Instead of setting me free, this book had diminished me and trapped me in false aspirations. It slayed the beast inside of me and left me completely toothless. With this book, I'd lost my bite. I'd lost my grip on the word. I'd lost Diane.

It wasn't worth it. As I walked down shamefully from one block to the other, coming in between the shadows of men and women who had forgotten how to live, robots running a prospering city, always green, always bigger, always more powerful, at the hands of people who have been resigned to a loop of eternal boredom and duty, something had pinched me. Something had irritated my bowels and reminded me I was a chosen member of the human race. I was born to write and hustle and claw.

And I had this book to show for it. This book—my book—was the culmination of the desire and effort I had gone through and endured to become a writer. To be published! To be known! To be read! And to throw it all away, now that I'm this close to my dream? What if the book ships in tomorrow? Next week? What if the sales suddenly skyrocket, and the book generates enough buzz and interest to become a best-seller, an instant hit? Writers with less talent were able to do it.

I decided to trade it all away. I decided I didn't want it anymore. I didn't want to be consigned to a life of enduring, of chasing a shadow I had created for myself. I wanted to write again, freely, even magnificently. I wanted to lay down the truth and make it sting. I wanted to look Diane in the eyes and kiss her bright-pink lips. I wanted to live.

The book had to go. Even if I never got my hands on another copy, even if this whole deal fell out tomorrow morning. I'd be alright with it.

I recognized Antoine's navy overall and matching navy shoes. I was wearing sagging jeans, which was good since my socks were unmatched. He greeted me like an old friend with a kind smile that could have been mistaken for compassion.

'So this is it?' he said. 'My copy's finally here?'

'Uh-huh. I had it pre-ordered for you. Special request. Couldn't leave a fan waiting for too long.'

'My, my, this is exciting! I'll finally get a chance to read you!'

'Yeah.'

I extended my arm and handed him the paper bag perched at its end. I couldn't even lift my face to oversee the transaction. Antoine took the bag, inspected it, took out the book, examined it, grimaced with his face, nodded, returned the book to the bag.

'How much do I owe you?' he said.

I allowed myself to be surprised by the question. In the midst of everything that had transpired, I was so caught up I'd forgotten to price the book. I couldn't call my publisher now and ask for the price at the risk of looking like a fool. It was too late to do anything.

'Well,' he said, 'are you going to tell me how much the book costs?'

I knew that if I told him I hadn't priced the book yet, he would never take me seriously and I would blow my only real chance of getting rid of my copy, despite some part of me still wanting to hold on to it and playing with my nerves. But I had to let it go. I knew there was no other way out for me.

Not thinking fully professionally, I allowed myself to blurt out, 'Just pay whatever you think it's worth.'

Fortunately for me, Antoine was a humorous man and decided to take my words light-heartedly instead of ridiculing me. 'You don't know what your work's worth? Come on, just tell me how much the book costs,' he said, laughing intermittently.

I thought asking a writer to value his own work was cruel and unfair. Everybody knew writers couldn't afford to overprice at the risk of losing their readers or getting shunned by potential buyers, and they certainly couldn't under-rate their work at the risk of underselling. The business world came with strict demands and regulations, and the writing and publishing sectors had to abide by those demands just like any other. There were no exceptions.

Antoine put me in a tough spot. I had no choice but to decide on a number and ask it from him. As he stood waiting for me to make up my mind, I replayed conversations with my publisher in my head and wondered how we never brought up a detail as important as this. The feeling of self-sabotage was prepared to haunt me for good if I failed at sealing this deal and continued in my steep spiraling descent.

Finally I gave him an answer. '30 euros,' I said. 'Fair?'

'You're selling your book for 30 euros?'

'Yeah,' I swallowed hard before answering.

'Very well then. A deal's a deal. I'm buying.'

He handed me the money. 3 papers of 10 euros each. It felt like laundered money.

Antoine thanked me for the book. Before parting, I told him, 'Take care of it, will you,' as if I was referring to a pet. He was right to look at me with confusion. He still acknowledged me with a nod and went his way. I folded the papers carefully and placed them in my pocket.

I felt light—strangely light—without my book. It was weighing on me like a boulder constantly strapped to my back.

Now in possession of financial power again, I caught the train and headed straight to the San Francisco bookstore.

I entered without looking at anybody and dashed to the FICTION section. I un-piled the stack of books lying next to the shelf and retrieved *Chump Change*. I felt my heart going from racing heartbeats to a steady-state.

I checkout out at the counter where the old keeper was sitting. I slammed the book in front of him and made him jump out of his seat. Before he had the chance to talk, I told him, 'Yes. I'm back. And guess what. I'm buying this book'.

I took out the 3 folded 10-euro bills from my pocket and placed them on the table. I unfolded them one by one while counting out loud, 'Ten…Twenty…Thirty'.

The shop owner was still trying to catch his breath. 'T-t-t-take the book,' he said. 'Just take the book and leave'.

'What about my change? I believe you said it's twenty-two fifty'.

I let him gather himself and find his feet again. His old arms were shaking and the veins were showing, bright fluid green blue little lines almost popping out of his skin.

He opened a drawer and took out a 5 euro bill, 2 1-euro pieces and a single 50-cents piece. 'Here's your money,' he said.

I gathered the change and the book and left. After so many defeats, this was a victory I was proud of.

I stopped outside and re-assessed myself after my performance in there, patting myself on the back for the win. I counted my money again, this time tallying up the total to plan my next investment. The amount was not enough to buy me alcohol, but I had enough for a train ticket to just about anywhere in the suburbs of Paris.

I decided to cash in on a ticket and catch a train to Diane's place. I stopped at my apartment first to tuck in my newest read on my writing desk and grab my notebook. I would have to finish my poem idea on the way to Diane's, I thought. My legs were all over the place, I felt like a kid at heart again, filled with exhilaration and hope and dreams. Something had kicked me in the gut, and a strange energy was flowing and amassing in the heart of my palms and radiating to my fingers.

I took the train while it was dark outside. The lights at the city's gates lit up the page in front of me as we exited Paris.

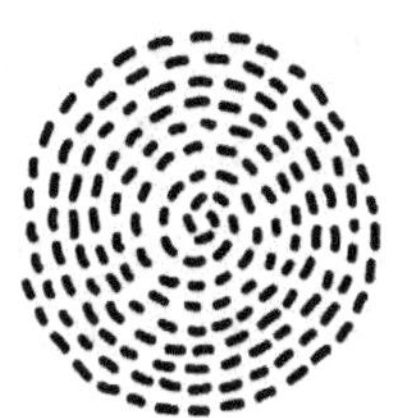

19

THE TRAIN RIDE WAS longer than usual and the train had to make unexpected stops. First, a passenger (a pregnant woman) got sick and the train had to be stopped and a small team of paramedics was rushed in to tend to her.

Then it was a bust-up between two black men that started with one of them shouldering the other for no apparent reason. They exchanged shoves which then turned into a brawl with several people forming a circle around them and making rowdy noises in the wagon. Again the train had to be stopped to break up the fight.

A third incident occurred when a passenger noticed an abandoned piece of baggage on a seat. The news spread in the train like wildfire and was met by streams of panic and howling concern by onboard travelers. The penalty was again a forced stop of the train and a delay at one of the stations for the suspicious package to be removed.

I was feeling very good about myself. I didn't let the train incidents derail me—on the contrary, I used the gained trip time to finish up my poem (which was starting to take shape). I had to stop between writing lines to observe the form, the coming-together on the page of the notebook. At the same time, darkness was gathering fast outside. The dark had always been kind to writers, serving as both a calming force and a muse to them. The shadows relaxed me and invited me to flex my finger muscles freely, extracting any and every bit of juice I had in my gut.

With my work almost done, and the train ride nearing its end, I started simulating my encounter with Diane. That brought back many things like the last time we met and fought. But it also brought back memories of sipping nights away and making love under the sheets with each a drink in our hand. Memories of her feeble breath as she clutched to my chest and ingrained her fingers in there sprouted and sprung from every corner of my mind. I felt myself starting to sweat involuntarily and started to crave a drink.

$\sim$

I had decided not to blow this. I tried to fight off the urge of alcohol quietly surging in me from the start. I thought cutting it off before it gained any room to build inside of me would put an end to it. But the quailing angst of the drink, the smell of a newly-opened bottle of whiskey was starting to appeal to my senses and call them out.

I realized thinking about Diane wasn't helping me. It made me more nervous, more gullible and more susceptible to the booze. I was an easy prey. I tried going over my poem again. But

I was sweating and shaking too much the lines in my pad started to jitter and jump around with me.

I thought about making a quick stop at a liquor store. Just for a quick one. I still had a bit of leftover cash on me. But my timing was all wrong and most places had already closed for the night.

There was a place not far from Diane's house that was open around the clock. The place came back to me as I relived habitual nocturnal walks with Diane, holding hands and smooching on the way from her house to the store. We'd buy out the place, stashing a week's worth of booze for the both of us and smoke for her.

I knew that place was my only chance to make it out alive tonight. My body was sending me distress signals I couldn't ignore. My legs were weary again and told me they were on the brink of letting me down. My heart was in a panic, sporadically disappearing completely and surging back to life with a pounding beat. My brain went dead. I looked on, through the window, through the scenes of trees and bushes and shrubs unwinding on each side of the tracks, then at the people, emptying themselves into their phones like bad old backups nobody was ever going to look at again.

Then the train stopped. I looked at the headboard and saw my destination light up in digitized orange letters. I was there.

I unrolled from the train out on the pavement and wobbled to the nearest vertical support. I was able to grab on to a sign pole to steady myself and adjust my posture. I wanted to compose myself and study my options. There was a hard decision to be made: make it to Diane's with a failing body or take the eight-mile to the liquor store a little further away?

20

I'D SUCCESSFULLY MANAGED TO make it out of the train station. As my body slouched toward the path that led from the station to Diane's house, I was still having trouble deciding whether to stop for alcohol first.

The darkness was heavy; the lampposts were out—I was even deprived of streetlights to guide me through my already difficult walk. Well, damn, I thought, and I could hear my entire body reciprocate that feeling.

I won't make it, I told myself. I won't make it to her house without a drink. At this point alcohol had stopped being a choice and had become an obligation. I pressed on, squeezing the blood into my paralyzed decaying legs that had let go. A few feet away from the apartment I spotted Diane's second-floor balcony. It showed no lights coming from the inside. But that didn't discourage me—I was determined to see her tonight no matter what. My body had other plans and was tilting toward that drink. I came close to the door but my body wasn't responding to my brain commands anymore. It kept working my legs and dragged on and away from the place.

I could only watch with helpless eyes another one of my masterful failures as my chances of seeing Diane were being swept away clean by my notorious alcoholism.

∽

I took the last steps forward and made it to the bar. My brain hadn't stopped harassing me all along the way with provocative talk and accusations—dismantling comments about how weak and finished as a person I was. When the logical hub of your body knew you were a loser, there wasn't much more you could hope for. The rest of me didn't care and was still after the elusive taste of the bottle.

As I prepared to enter I couldn't help but notice the place was darker than usual. There didn't appear to be any people, but there was no indication or sign anywhere on the front door. I tried to force the door. It wouldn't open. I tried knocking. Nobody answered. I tried forcing again. The damn thing wouldn't budge.

I went around and finally caught a small sign on one side of the bar. The sign was written in print on a little page stitched on the top left corner.

<u>NOTICE:</u> WE NOW CLOSE ON SUNDAYS. THANK YOU FOR YOUR UNDERSTANDING.

Knowing my luck, I guessed it was a Sunday. I read the sign again and moved back to the front of the bar to make sure. They were closed.

My lips started to wobble. I couldn't tell if it was the lack of alcohol or pure shame. How could I face Diane after this? After choosing booze over her? After ending up empty-handed, with a broken body that had trouble standing straight and a broken mind that seemed determined to torture me?

I turned around and walked back with my hands in my pockets. I felt the wriggling paper crushed at the bottom of my right pocket. I took it out and remembered it was the poem I wrote. It didn't seem to have as much value now but it was all I had. I straightened the page and folded it geometrically before gently putting it back in my pocket. I decided to use whatever energy my body had left to go back to Diane's. I moved, grabbing on to every wall, pole, edge, tree, thinking of the night, the cold, the city, life, the word, love, the finality of it all. Love, the finality of it all.

I made it to Diane's place. It took a moment of hesitation, followed by a thousand more of roaring courage to knock on that door. I heard little footsteps. She opened.

Diane was shocked.

'Listen,' I told her, 'I know this is bad timing and a surprise to you, but I can explain.'

'What do you want?'

'I want us back together, Diane. I've had it with the fights and the sleepless nights and the lonely all-day blues. I love you. I love you and I'm sorry. You were right. I'm a bad fuck-up. I let myself go so deep I couldn't find my way back. And all because of what? Some minor success. A book. A single book.'

'But isn't your book selling?' she said in a skeptical voice.

'Selling?' I said. 'Ha! My book hasn't even shipped yet.'

'Why's that?'

'I'm not sure. And I don't really care. The point is, Diane, I want to try again. I want to stop this tidal mess crashing down on me. I made something I want to share with you. A poem.'

I took out my page and read it to her. I read slowly, with eloquence, articulating each word in my mouth for full effect. When I was finished, I held the paper close to my chest, like an artist proud of his work who'd just shared the intimacy of his art with the rest of the world for the first time.

Diane looked less than impressed. 'Listen,' she said, 'if you think a poem is going to win me back, then you've just wasted your time.'

'Diane, wait,' I said. 'I didn't read you the poem to win you back. I read it to you to show you I was serious at being a writer again. That I could commit myself to writing. I sold my only copy of my book and spent my time working on this poem.'

'You sold your only copy of your book? Why?'

'I couldn't have it hanging around me anymore. That thing wasn't doing me any good. It was poisoning my mind, making me too proud to even play at being a writer. I stopped writing. And you know what happens to writers who stop writing.'

'I'm curious though,' she said. 'What did you do with the money?'

'I bought a book,' I told her. 'Something to read and maybe get moved by.'

She smiled. It was the purest smile I'd seen on a human face in a long time.

'Diane,' I told her, 'I don't know how long it will take you to forgive me and accept me, but you have here standing a man fighting on two fronts: as a writer and a lover. The writer is chasing after his scattered words, and the lover is pursuing his lost love. And for once, I would like to be an all-around winner. I would like to be a serial winner and win my battles.'

She took the poem from my hand and read it. 'This is the winner,' she said, holding the paper in my face. 'This is the winner I've been desperately trying to hold on to. This is the man I don't want to lose. Tell me, John, am I going to lose you again?'

I looked at her imploring eyes and forgot my body. I forgot the alcohol and the thumping pain and the shivers and the torturing thoughts my brain had been sending me. It was like I'd decided to switch everything off, get rid of all the lights and just sit in darkness with Diane holding a candle up to me. I knew the word had done me a favor with the universe and earned me that second shot. I imagined my poem a shockwave diffusing in ripples, touching every part of my life and bringing it all back full circle.

I held her hands tightly and pressed them with mine. Then I pulled her close and planted a kiss on her forehead. 'You won't,' I said. 'Writer's honor.'

She giggled. It was that same giggle that made me fall for her the first time around.

'So,' she said, cheeks flushed, her right foot drawing circles on the floor, 'what happens now?'

'Well, I could use a drink.'

'I can make some coffee,' she said, throwing in another smile.

'Coffee sounds great.'

Diane made coffee. We sat and drank our cups, our eyes meeting each other at every sip, not tilting, not waving away, making sure to always find each other in the dark, while outside everything receded and began again.

I put on some piano music and we turned off the lights. Diane lit a candle and grabbed her cup and sat next to me. Chopin came on and started playing, reviving everything I remembered was pleasant to me.

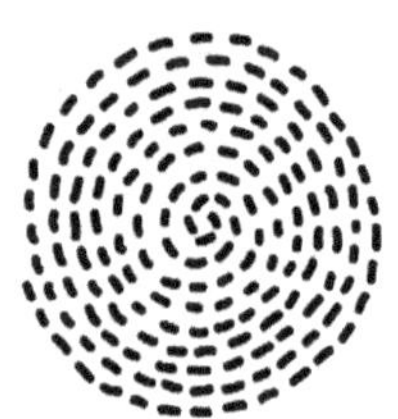

21

I **KNEW AN ARTIST** that only painted on the side of buildings. He would scale them and draw paintings of monuments, historical figures, sometimes emboldened words in explosive graffiti art. Many people tried to make him hold a brush and stand in front of a white canvas but he never could. He would only paint on buildings, saying, 'This is the only way to show my art to the world!'

Each artist had his madness. But I thought painters were treated better than writers. I thought they had it easier. It took a lot more from people to carry books and read them. It required more time, more energy than just looking at art.

Paintings were easy. They were breathless, effortless. They didn't ask much of people except observation. With writing it was different. You needed imagination. You needed visualization. You needed breath and stamina to follow up with the chain of words and the flipping of the pages.

And for the writer, you needed flair. Good artists generally had good hands. They weren't all talented, just meticulous and good with details. You couldn't cut it like that as a writer. You needed more. To write you needed your toes to dance, to shiver at night under the sheets when you're being stalked by a line that's carving your skull open. You needed music, colors, rhythm. You needed soul.

Diane and I were happy. We made love for 10 straight days, several times a day. I'd almost forgotten what groping her perfect ass felt like. How it fell perfectly on either side of those linen underwear of hers (the velvet ones were my favorite). Making love to Diane was like writing—godlike, supreme, miraculous. It was filled with piano and jazz music that pierced our naked skins. Diane glowed every time her body slipped under mine. I enjoyed groping her thighs while her legs curled around my spine.

After sex, we indulged in a moment of pure silence, staring at each other and smiling. She would occasionally giggle. Then I'd get up and get us both ice cream from the freezer. Raspberry chocolate. Our favorite.

Meanwhile the writing was going well. I had several new poems lined up for Diane to read. She reveled in them. She read each one several times with a different voice. When she was done with it, she'd lean in and kiss me. 'My handsome writer,' she would whisper.

I was growing back into my skin. I had forgotten about my book, about the shipping, about the sales. Or maybe I hadn't. I had simply decided to stop caring. My publisher tried to get in touch with me many times, but the phone always sent him to voicemail. He left me several voice messages, most of which I deleted without listening to. At the end of every month, I received a nice sales report from him with my share of earnings highlighted at the bottom of the page.

I never looked at those but Diane did, reading them to herself with a little smile and then patting me on the back while I was busy writing away on my computer.

I wrote furiously, hungrily. But I still had the money problem. I had skipped a couple of months' rent (and electricity) at my apartment but it was okay since I had moved back with Diane. But her job wasn't enough for the both of us and it didn't take me long to understand I wasn't going to be paying bills anytime soon with any writing money, even if my output had dramatically increased.

I needed a job.

As a proud non-working man, I hated the philosophy of work. Somehow it fell between the lines of capitalism and exploitation for me. I could never dissociate the idea of work from slavery or find any redeeming qualities in it. Working to pay the bills wasn't a convincing argument for me. There were starved artists on the streets of Paris who sat barefoot on the sidewalk to sketch tourists all day. Those were the ones in need of work the most and they weren't out looking for it.

I started looking for jobs. I wanted to be smart about this and try to zone in on something that would make use of my skillset instead of randomly applying for job ads stapled on street polls or on the side of a dentist's office.

Since I didn't have much of an education or noteworthy experience to mention in a résumé, Diane suggested I make a list of my strengths (or 'hire points', as she liked to call them).

I ripped out a page from my poem book and started scheming about the possible attributes I could put down. Nothing came to mind. It became apparent to me that I had in fact, during my lifespan, failed to pick up a single trait that would make me 'hireable' by a company. Nobody in the corporate world would take a down-and-out writer seriously let alone consider him for a position.

I'd hit a wall again. This time my incompetence was biting me in the ass like an angry piranha. I had no options.

But then I thought about it: how many candidates could boast being bum writers? How many of them could share the experience I had amassed over years of writing, rejection and heartbreak? If that didn't stand out enough to get me an interview, then at least it would make for an interesting story to whomever would gamble on my name inside an office.

Embracing my bold revelation, I went through the job revolving door and joined the pool of dimwitted aspiring workers looking for employment.

I sent my information left and right, making sure to leave a contact number everywhere (in Diane's words, 'Always make sure you're reachable, you never know where your break could come from,' which I chose to believe). But the process was slow. For some reason, companies weren't as enthusiastic to hire as candidates were to get hired. They'd let them eat each other's heads off if it meant giving them the time to see ONE MORE applicant.

I wasn't good with waiting. But waiting for answers for a potential job was easier than waiting for the inspiration to write, I found. At least there was some movement there: some phone calls from human resources saying you're not a good fit, some exchanged emails going back and forth before hitting a dead-end, even on-site interviews with several people wearing expensive shiny suits asking you questions you should have memorized the answers for.

The wait for writing was different. It left you brain-dead a good amount of time and watched your mind rot and get chewed on by the worms long enough to decompose. Then one day, when you didn't have the strength to get out of the sheets or stand the sun, it poked you.

I didn't want to be rattled by any kind of wait. So I decided to approach it the same way I had in the past: by drinking. I slumped into drunkenness, mostly on wine and beer. Diane would drink with me some nights, but she'd shaken off the alcohol spree that had possessed her for so long. When I couldn't write, we went to the movies, we read in the park, we filled the house with music. Diane even sang sometimes and put on a performance to make me feel better.

I tried to get out of it. I tried to be different from any other human being waiting on a decision he had no say in. But it was hard. The job, the money, the responsibility. Why couldn't I be discovered by some underground agent in a bar in Paris who'd offer to pay me to quit everything and write for the rest of my life?

I would gladly take the responsibility of my words, of making more of them, of making volumes of them for the rest of my existence. But the 9-to-6 was one of the worst atrocities invented by mankind, and I could feel my soul rejecting it more and more with every drop of booze.

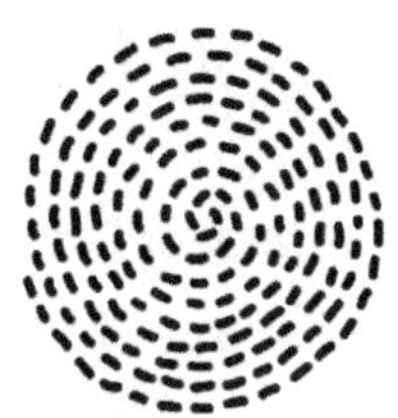

22

I WAS AWAKENED BY a phone call, half-drenched in a puddle of sweat and wine stains. It was noon. Diane was at work. The house was eerily quiet after endless nights of music.

It turned out the calling number was from one of the companies I had applied for. They had seen my profile and wanted to arrange a meeting. I managed to sober myself up just enough to agree on a personal interview in two days. The lady on the phone thanked me and wished me a great day.

Later that day I broke the news to Diane when she came back home. She jumped in my arms and started kissing me everywhere. 'We should celebrate,' I told her. 'Let's go out.'

We went to a bar not far from the house. Diane was wearing a yellow summer dress and white shoes. She hopped along the way in front of me, occasionally turning back to smile at my face.

'You're going to get a job, you're going to get a job,' she sang.

We made it to the bar and found our seats. Diane ordered a Belgian beer while I went with a whiskey-and-coke. She looked at me with shining eyes, still raving about the news.

'Baby,' I said, 'it's just an interview. There's no guarantee I'm getting the job.'

'But I'm sure you will! The fact that out of all the companies you applied to, those guys showed interest in you! That's a sign! It's the opportunity I've been telling you to look out for!'

Maybe Diane was right. Maybe the job hunt was all about luck. All it took was the right pair of eyes to set on your profile and boom, you were the potential next hotshot to walk into your very own cubicle. What I sensed though was that Diane had much more faith in me than I did in myself. I tried to set her expectations.

'Listen, I don't want you to get your hopes up for this interview. I'm sure they've got a lot of other guys who are more qualified than me and who are interviewing for the same job. I don't want you to end up disappointed. If it doesn't work out, there'll be other jobs.'

She nodded happily. I could tell she didn't believe it and was just trying to please me.

It was the day of the interview and I unceremoniously made my way past the front door of the company. I arrived late and tipsy from the beers I hammered on the way over. I was wearing a clean shirt that I'd forgotten to iron and that made my entire body look like it had been run over by a truck.

Before making it to the reception desk, I made a quick right to the bathroom and applied water on my hair to make it look straighter. I thought it would take the attention off my wrinkled shirt.

Then I strutted back to the front desk, jacked hair miraculously standing together with water, creased shirt, and pants that hadn't been washed for over a month.

'Excuse me,' I said to the receptionist, 'I have an appointment with Mrs. Flower?'

'It's Mrs. Flauder,' she said. 'Third door on the left.'

Mrs. Flauder was a sassy blonde woman in her forties. She wasn't married and had powdered her face so much she looked like a revenant. She greeted me with an attempted smile she had trouble keeping because of all the Botox restricting her cheeks.

We sat down and she pulled out a file from under the table. She opened it and started going through some papers. Then she read my profile, making sure to stop at every piece of information for validity from my end. I said yes to all, still feeling a bit dazed and sulking in my white oval chair.

'We're very pleased to have you here, Mr. Kaliba,' she said.

'Please, call me John.'

'Very well, John. First let me ask you, how are you feeling? Are you relaxed?'

'As a matter of fact I am.'

'I want you to be very relaxed. This interview is just standard procedure. Nothing to worry about.'

'Oh, yes, I'm very relaxed.'

'Good. Do you know what this interview's for?'

'To discuss my job application.'

'Actually, no. That's why we brought you here. There's been a change…'

'What kind of change?'

'Well, actually, I don't know how to say this. Oh shoot, I'm just going to tell you. You haven't been selected for the position.'

'Then why am I here?'

'Because we thought you'd fit in well in another vacancy we have.'

'What kind of vacancy?'

'It says here you're a writer. Correct?'

'Correct.'

'So you're good with language and words?'

'Actually, a writer isn't…'

'Fantastic! I'll just write that down: Good with words.'

'Excuse me.'

'Yes?'

'I'm confused.'

'About what, John?'

'About the job. The new job.'

'What about it?'

'What exactly will I be doing?'

'Oh, silly me! We're actually looking for a linguist. Someone who's good with grammar and language structure. You see, a big part of our work is done by machines. We rely heavily on them to generate a lot of text, like say, financial reports. What we need is someone to validate that text.'

'Uh-huh.'

'With your profile as a writer, I thought who better than him for this role! So, what do you say?'

'Listen, thanks for the offer, but I'm not exactly…'

'Here's how much you'll be making.'

Mrs. Flauder took out a small piece of paper and jotted a number on it. There were a lot of zeroes in there.

When she showed me the number, I thought about the rent. I thought about the electricity bill. I thought about Diane and how proud she would be. It was like something had swept in and erased all the atrocities of the job. It felt nice being an employee and getting to work early every day.

'I'll take it,' I said.

She had me sign a contract. She also handed me a small booklet that looked like a cheque book.

'It's a lunch booklet,' she explained. 'Every ticket in there lets you buy a prepaid meal. On the house, of course. Or should I say on the company.'

I took the booklet and shook her hand again before leaving. 'You start tomorrow,' Mrs. Flauder said. 'We have a backlog of work ready for you and we certainly don't want to lose time.'

But even that didn't faze me. I felt powerful, very powerful with what I was just offered. It felt like power had been handed down to me. The gods were smiling at last at my fortunes. To sit in a desk 9 hours a day and get paid for it and eat for free! I felt the writer in me shaming himself. There was nothing writing could offer compared to this.

I smiled at the lady one last time. 'Just curious here,' I said, still a little light-headed, 'I was wondering what position I had applied for when I sent in my profile.'

'You'd applied for the accountant vacancy. Surely a mistake on your behalf. I don't see any economy, finance or mathematics in your background that would've made you suitable for that job. But lucky for you we were able to place you where we think your skills will be utilized best.'

'Yeah.'

She escorted me to the door. I could hear my father's voice cackling in my ear. I had upstaged the old man and gotten a better job than anything he had put together his entire life by working half as much. I was beginning to look at the other side of the coin. I was playing with a different set of marbles.

The sun blew me away with its rays. My face soaked in it. I walked to the train station with a signed contract under my arm and caressing the small lunch booklet in my hands.

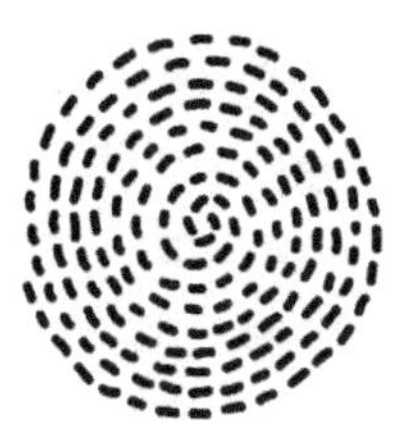

23

THE NEXT DAY I was led into a glass cubicle with a small desk and a laptop sitting on it. I was instructed to: never bring or use hardware that was my own, always notify (verbally and in writing) the company of any absence ONE day prior, take one-hour lunch breaks only (no other breaks were allowed during working hours).

I was shown around the physical and virtual environments I would work in. A quick visit to the other cubicles accompanied by a small introduction of people whose names I would never remember constituted the fastest tour I'd ever been part of. After that a short demo on my workstation and a verbal listing of all the commands (which I would also never remember) I would use during my work were passed on to me in the form of a dictated college lab session.

After the INITIATION (the term used by the company) was over, I was finally left alone in my cubicle. First I stared at the laptop. The guy showing me everything had left it running some batch commands that popped up horizontally in rows on the black screen. I understood there had been a text there somewhere, on some part of my screen, which I couldn't locate, mostly because it didn't resemble any form of English I had run into my entire life. The text was supposedly in some byte format—which meant it didn't look anything like a text or a corpus of words. At least, that was what I caught from the guy's explanation. The text was supposedly being analyzed by some advanced sophisticated algorithm, and I had to monitor and supervise the analysis and evaluate its accuracy.

I looked at the thing again. It kept going. I'd never seen a computer screen filled with so much jargon. My personal typer, in comparison, had trouble booting up and loading a blank document for me to write actual text on.

The machine was still going. It was going in a frenzy. It felt like it was overwhelming itself. Unnecessarily even, I thought. It could damn well take a small break. I, simple human, was allowed a one-hour break and I worked much less than that thing. But then again, I didn't want to interrupt its work.

I let the thing roll on. I sat back in my comfortable chair and played with the handles on the sides, experimenting with different sitting positions. Then I re-imagined last night, coming back home a winner. I thought about opening the door, waving my contract high above my head to Diane, babbling, singing, showing her my stack of free lunch tickets. Diane looked at me with pride. 'You made it,' she said, kissing me, 'We made it.' She later whispered that to me all night as we made love to vanilla-scented candles and Mozart.

'Who said writers are tough to deal with?' I told her. 'Writers own the fucking world!'

She giggled. Her laughter filled space and disintegrated into beautiful little stars.

The warmth of last night came back to me and made the hairs on my hands stand up. I'd punched my ticket into the corporate world and was feeding off its rewards like a parasite. I understood why people got hooked to it, why they accepted it.

The glory of what I felt made me want to take a nap. I wanted to extend and preserve this feeling a little longer. I drew my eyes to the screen and saw it was still spitting logs at a frenetic speed, so I pushed my head back against the chair and rested my eyes.

I woke up an hour or so later. The machine was idle, there in front of me. It had finished its computations. I decided it was time for my lunch break.

The firm was ideally located in a busy neighborhood in the Parisian area. The streets were littered with restaurants and food stands. I walked past them, driven by my growling stomach and wet salivating mouth. I was having a hard time adjusting to the reality that I had a say in what kind of food I ate for the first time. No more counting pennies! My pockets were free of them, and they were happier that way. My stomach leaped and turned at the idea of not having to settle for a tasteless ham and cheese sandwich, and my taste glands raved in the new choices that suddenly opened up to them.

I made full usage of my time, stopping anywhere I thought would make an interesting culinary experience, reading the menu, asking questions, interactively engaging with whoever was at the forefront of the place. I allowed myself to appreciate food the same way I appreciated music: slowly, and passionately.

My explorations led me to a small stand that specialized in wraps. The setup attracted me: there were two Indian men, one in charge of taking orders, the other preparing them. They had a big old gas oven with a spherical surface placed in between them, like the ones used to make Pita bread in Levantine countries.

I checked out the menu hanging above their heads. They'd only written the names of the wraps, without any mention of their constituents. They had 5 or 6 different types to choose from. I decided to be adventurous and just pick one without asking any questions.

The man at the cash register greeted me. He asked me what I wanted to eat. I checked the menu again. 'I'll have a Parisian wrap,' I told him in a commanding voice.

He smiled at me and communicated the order to the other Indian who activated himself and started working on the dough.

With my food getting ready I decided to switch off. I thought about the office again. About going back to that cubicle and sitting in front of that machine. It felt very different from sitting in front of the typer on my writing desk. My body started to itch for unknown reasons, and I felt a kind of cold pain scalding me, as if someone was sliding a hot metal rod down my body.

I thought about pushing away whatever negative vibe my body had picked up and focus on the food instead. With the order ready, the first Indian totaled me. '12 euros, please,' he said.

Proudly, I reached into my jacket pocket and took out my full lunch booklet. I opened it and flipped through the tickets inside. They were all identical. I selected the last ticket in the book and carefully took it out, making sure to rip along the dotted lines printed on the margin. I handed the man the ticket. He gave me my wrap.

I held the thing in both hands. It was huge. The still-hot bread was coming together, closing in against the ingredients inside as if wanting to fuse with them into one layer of food. I had to take a deep breath before taking the first bite with my gaping mouth.

I closed my eyes and tasted. I savored the wrap as if it were high-class French cuisine. It was saucy, and I could make out a lot of the ingredients in it: tomatoes, corn, pickles. But I couldn't identify the base. Was it chicken? Meat? It could've been either, a good sauce could make them both taste the same.

I went back to the Indian at the register. 'Excuse me,' I said. 'What's inside this wrap?'

'Oh, many things sir. Tomatoes, corn, pickles…'

'No, I mean the base. What's the base ingredient? Chicken? Meat?'

He went quiet for a second.

'Sir, it's ham and cheese.'

He kept talking after that. But I didn't hear him. His voice and the rest of the noise in the street were flushed and warped out of existence. I was floating in limbo, and everyone and everything around me turned invisible. Engulfed by a great white. No background. I was alone.

I still had my sandwich in hand. It looked like a mess, but it seemed more familiar now. I recognized the chunks of ham stamped on the layer of bread and the melted cheese spilling out of it. I reached for my jacket and pulled out my little booklet. I flipped it and counted. I had 30 tickets left, enough to buy me lunch for the entire month. But all that was void now. All that had brought me full circle.

The taste of freedom, the enjoyment brought by buying my own food or eating anything I wanted seemed much less significant and dissipated in a cloud of truth I had ignored up until now. I had impersonated an employee, I had taken the place of a corporate worker. The searing flashes of pain came back to my body wanting out of this shell that was holding it hostage.

The fancy cubicle and the lunch tickets weren't good for me. They weren't the grind I was after. That machine waiting for me at the office would have to keep doing work on its own. There was nothing I could contribute in there, or anywhere else for that matter.

The only place for me was the writing desk, the dark room, the mad walls, the floor with Diane by my side.

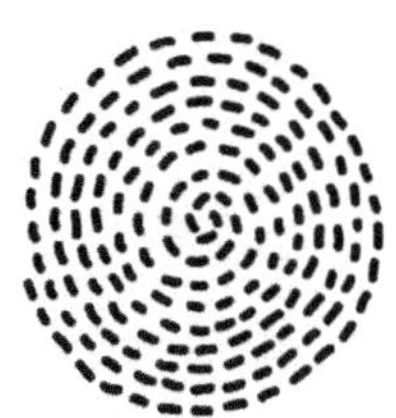

24

I WASN'T GOING TO be a hero. They weren't going to get a speech out of me. I ate up my sandwich and returned to the office.

The computer at my desk was brooding. I looked at it once, twice, sat in my chair, clicked on some unclosed windows, tried to read some open documents and other files that could have been useful. I was wasting my time.

I closed the damn thing shut and went back to see Mrs. Flauder. I didn't have anything prepared to say to her except the obvious: I was done. I didn't want the job, I didn't want the perks, I didn't want the bright future. I wanted to sit in one place and write and continue to honor that act so many greats had busted their lives in half for.

Mrs. Flauder was eating a salad on her desk. She was surprised to see me striding forward, both determined and fully sober this time. She put down her plate.

Before she could speak, I blurted out whatever words my mind had prepared and chained them in sentences.

'I'm done. I can't work here. I can't do this job. This isn't right. This isn't right for me.'

Despite Mrs. Flauder's best efforts to follow, understand and try to calm me down and correlate whatever I was feeling with Imposter Syndrome, everything in me wouldn't listen.

My hands were shaking. My legs were tired. I wanted to leave after one half-day at the job. I did my best to take out the ticket book and return it without shaking my hands. I failed miserably.

I dragged the booklet from my jacket across my stomach right onto the table because my fingers and articulations were letting me down badly. Mrs. Flauder smiled and pushed the book away, insisting I keep it.

Then I let myself go. I let the shaking get a hold of me, I let the fear and the worry tighten my neck and strap it with a wire, I let the uncertainty of my near future kick in. The money, the bills, Diane. The same recurrent pattern. I was the ungrateful sonofabitch who refused the escape rope life had thrown him.

Nothing made sense. This was the real world, the world where jobs and paychecks happened. The world where a week of poverty could send you down 7 hells. You could be buried alive, you could be eaten up and nobody would move. The trees wouldn't move for you.

In a short respite, I was allowed to breathe by my cramping chest. A little touch in me told me one person in the world still believed in the way I saw things. That person had advocated me to write more mercilessly than any voice that inhabited me over the years.

I decided to believe in that thought like a mad prayer of salvation. I shook my head to Mrs. Flauder, blurting to her it was unnecessary and futile to try to talk me through it. My mind, my body and the rest of me were made up. I was going home.

I exited the premises with the booklet in hand. The shaking had stopped. I called Diane and told her everything that happened. She remained silent throughout the conversation. I told her that I quit my job, that I was going to be a full-time writer, that everything was going to be okay. Then I told her I was taking her out to dinner tonight. She was happy. We were going to make it.

On the train ride back, I was thinking about wrapping Diane in my arms. About making endless love to her. About the urge to write. I looked outside the window. We were crossing the Seine. There was an infectious blueness in the water I hadn't noticed before.

About the Author

HANNA ABI AKL IS a Lebanese-born English writer. He lived in Beirut before moving to France in 2018. Hanna writes contemporary poetry and prose. His writing continues to be heavily featured in literary magazines, poetry journals and anthologies. Hanna has already published his debut novel, *A Road Away From Home* (2017), as well as two poetry collections, *Diary In Poems* (2018) and *Vitality* (2019).